BEATRICE
AT BAY

BOOK TWO OF
THE BEATRICE
· MCILVAINE
ADVENTURE
SERIES

by Bruce and Carson
McCandless

BEATRICE
AT BAY

What I want is Facts. Teach these boys and girls nothing but Facts. Facts alone are wanted in life. Plant nothing else, and root out everything else.

Charles Dickens

It is not light that we need, but fire; it is not the gentle shower, but thunder. We need the storm, the whirlwind, and the earthquake.

Frederick Douglass

One: The Content of Clouds

Not long after the death of her dad, Beatrice McIlvaine was tormented by visions of doom in the shape of a dream-eating dragon. This lizard had sail-sized, leathery wings. It had teeth that could shred a sheep, and it was hunting her. Every evening the creature set out in search of her blood. Every night as she slept, Beatrice saw the monster a little more clearly, and a little closer to her home. She knew what it wanted. It wanted her dead. It wanted her family dead and it wanted to leave their little house a smoking heap of hair and ashes.

She ignored her head for as long as she could, hoping the visions would go away on their own. But they didn't. They got bigger and louder and more intense until they drove her out of her bedroom and into the scrubby field beyond her backyard, where she stood screaming at the sky in frustration and fear. And finally she decided to fight the dragon, with help from a mysterious but kindly middle-aged woman named Inocencia Knowles who looked a little like Angela Lansbury and who was at various times a math teacher, a gym coach, and a cafeteria lady, though she wasn't particularly good at being any of these things.

Mrs. Knowles gave Beatrice a mystical horse and an enchanted sword. They were almost enough. In the end, though, Beatrice needed the assistance of her fiercely protective mother and her very unmagical cat to put an end to the giant reptile. It was a brilliant and mystifying moment: the wind in her mouth like the night's secret name, terror dancing alive like lightning in her veins. In the skies above muddy Galveston Bay, on the back of a horse with wings, she slammed the sword so deep into the monster's chest that the creature fell from the heavens in a 500-foot plume of fire.

And things got better.

That's what you want to hear, right? Hey, if this was a Disney movie, you could rest assured, knowing that Beatrice and her mom, Anne, and her little brother, Frankie, learned to cherish each other. That they resigned themselves to the tragic death of Beatrice's dad. That they moved into a two-story townhouse right there at the corner of Innocence and Honesty, attractively furnished with a mudroom, infinity pool, and electric labradoodle.

But this ain't Disney.

And that didn't happen.

In fact, the McIlvaine household looked a lot like it always had. Beatrice, Anne, and Frankie still lived in the same dumpy duplex on Belgrove Avenue. Anne had money problems—or, more precisely, *not-enough-money* problems. Frankie had a temper. Beatrice felt awkward and indistinct and wished she had more friends, especially after her bestie Jennifer Ramos moved to the north side of Houston, fifty miles away. They kept in touch on Snapchat, so Jennifer could still tell Beatrice what to wear and how to layer her foundation, but it wasn't the same. Beatrice missed her.

Admittedly, some things got better. Frankie, now thirteen, was less manic. He'd scaled way back on his search for elusive pirate treasures buried in the sticky red clay of coastal Texas, even if he occasionally couldn't resist, and dug out his headphones and metal detector and went traipsing through public parks and private backyards, oblivious to the strange looks he was getting. He had friends—weird, sticky friends, but friends nevertheless. He went to school most days, and some days he actually stayed there. His math grades were impressive, if erratic, and occasionally he joined his family for dinner.

Beatrice's mom no longer cleaned stalls and fed horses at the Flying D Stables. She was now the office manager for Cooper's Large Animal Veterinary Clinic at the corner of Dyckman and 146. This meant she was indoors most of the time, and worked regular hours. She kept food on the table. And she thought she was falling in love.

A thirty-eight-year-old woman. In *love*.

Creepy, right? More on this later.

Anne McIlvaine was a realist. She missed her husband, who'd died four years ago in an accident that sometimes seemed so unreal to her that she found herself desperate to wake up from whatever bad dream had suggested it. She ached for the warmth of Patrick McIlvaine's smile. She longed for the snow-pack strength of his shoulders and the comfort of his indestructible optimism. Still, she knew she couldn't bring him back, and she was one of those people who could relive an emotion without letting it own her.

Her kids?

Not so much.

Beatrice was a freshman in high school.

It wasn't as disgusting as junior high. She'd give it that much. She didn't have any close friends in her classes, but the kids were better groomed and slightly less annoying. Most of them had learned to manage or conceal their odd odors and behavioral quirks, and were trying to figure out how to deal with the demons in their own heads rather than constantly picking on each other. There was just less *drama* in high school, and this helped. More importantly, the school itself was bigger and brighter and so crowded that Beatrice felt liberated, in an odd sort of way. She'd never met most of the people she saw in the halls, and she didn't feel any particular need to meet them now. She knew she didn't exactly fit in after the dragon incident. She knew she might never fit in again, but she appreciated the feeling of moving in groups, of flowing where the crowd flowed, of being part of some larger organism.

Her classmates seemed to feel the same way. They weren't particularly friendly, but they weren't unpleasant either. They left her alone. So she did her thing. She was a choir geek, and practiced singing to millions of fans—sometimes with Jennifer while FaceTiming, at other times, late at night, all alone. She played second-string point guard on the girls' basketball team. She slept most nights without dodging bad dreams, and she managed to keep her GPA at a solid if not exactly stellar level. English was an easy A. Math was a sweaty B. Worse, if she wasn't careful.

Beatrice talked more these days. She occasionally smiled when she listened to her music. But she had her blue times too, times when she sat in the backyard and stared out over the open field that belonged to the water district at nothing in particular. Her home in Seabrook was only three miles from the Gulf of Mexico. It was therefore directly under the flight path of a more or less constant stream of mountainous cumulus clouds. The clouds argued with each other as they traveled north. They rose and fell and reconfigured themselves to make lumpy sketches in the sky, birds and bears and the heads of presidents and pop stars, and sprawled on a lawn chair Beatrice would watch the pageant and feel herself hit by giant waves of longing and regret and a sadness that had no outer edges. She would think of her fireman father, hero of all her childhood dreams, who died on the side of a freeway as she watched him bleed. She'd recall her beloved cat, Alexander the Great, and wonder what lay just beyond the lip of the blue realm above. And occasionally she felt currents of anger moving within her, even though she'd been through a whole lot of counseling and was meant to have developed coping skills and girls were supposed to be able to get over these things, and when that clenched black sensation came the sky seemed to swirl with her own frustration that her father was gone and now Jennifer Ramos too and that no one at school seemed to know she was alive and that her mother was increasingly wrapped up in her relationship with a man Beatrice barely knew and didn't particularly care for.

After an hour or two Beatrice would grow restless. People would come out of neighboring houses and start pointing at the heavens as if something really bad was about to happen, and Beatrice would stop her brooding. She didn't want to scare anyone. The shapes in the sky became vague again as the clouds uncoupled and quit listening to her. It was as if she could only float in the sadness for a limited time. Then it would spit her back out, like a foreign body—one of the living, not suitable for extended communion with souls that had passed. At times like this she needed to do something. Run. Wash dishes. Shoot fifty baskets.

And that's how Beatrice wound up on the asphalt basketball courts of Ed White Elementary School, her alma mater, a flat-roofed single-story structure named for the Apollo 1 astronaut who was the first American to walk in space.

The sun was sinking in the west as she practiced free throws. *Even stance. Three dribbles. Ball on the tips of the fingers.* Despite her concentration, she noticed the van as soon as it pulled up. It was seventy-five yards away, parked at the edge of the playground where a barbed wire fence separated school property from an overgrown pasture. JOHNSON PLUMBING, said the lettering on the side of the vehicle.

WE'LL STOP YOUR GRIPES
ABOUT YOUR PIPES

It was only a few minutes later, when she heard shouting coming from the vehicle, that Beatrice went to investigate. She kept her distance, of course. This was beyond sketchy. This was a van without windows, parked at the edge of an empty field. Someone was shouting inside it. In fact, it was possible *two* someones were shouting inside it. It was the classic van abduction scenario. But she was fit, and on familiar ground, and she needed to know what was happening. Besides, the voices she heard belonged to kids.

"Help us!" one called.

"Go away!" said another.

But the "Help us!" was louder.

Two: She Doesn't Believe Them

"Tell me again?" said Beatrice. She tried to see past the faces in the front seat of the van. It was no use. Too dark.

"We already told you," said the van's driver. He had coppery skin and long black hair that curtained his forehead. A wispy beard clung to his chin. He was maybe sixteen years old. But his eyes were older.

"That's why I said *again*. Because I'm still not sure I believe you."

"Fine," said the girl in the passenger seat, leaning over to get a better look at Beatrice. She had short hair dip-dyed blue, along with matte, patchy dark eyeshadow paired with smudged liner. And an odd accent. Russian, maybe. She seemed to be the one in charge here. Or the one who wanted to be in charge. She looked—and sounded—dangerous. "*Don't* believe. That is going both ways, basketball person."

"Forget it, Lester," said someone from the back. Beatrice could see a little better now. It was another male. There were three kids back there. Two boys and a girl. The girl was chewing bubble gum. "She doesn't care. Let's bounce."

"Dude, chill. I wouldn't believe us either." The driver shrugged and gazed at Beatrice again through his waterfall bangs. She recognized the look in his eyes. It was exhaustion—coupled with fear. She knew a bit about both. "But I'm telling you the truth. We escaped."

"*Escaped?*"

"From a school. A school that's more like a prison."

"From a school. I got that part. Like Hogwarts, for smart kids."

Smart, *greasy* kids, Beatrice wanted to add. But she bit her tongue.

"Hogwarts," said the girl in the passenger seat, holding her cigarette out the window to flick the ash, "is allegory. It may seem like fantasy about cuddly witch people. In reality, it is fable meant to justify outdated notions of socio-economic predestination and class privilege."

Yes. The accent. Definitely Russian. It made it hard to figure out if her ws were vs, and vice versa. "Witch" sounded waguely like *vitch*.

"Mila!" said a voice from the back. "Not again."

"Shut up, Sanjay," said the blue-haired girl. "Wizards represent upper class, *mudbloods* their half-breed intermediaries, and *muggles* the rest of beer-swilling, football-stupid British public. You can't *work* your way into wizard class, correct, boy-like redheaded girl?"

"Who? Me?"

"You are only boy-like redhead in vicinity, yes? If in fact you are truly redhead."

"Hey. You're getting a little—"

"LABOR CONVEYS NO BENEFITS! Mumbo-jumbo sorcery juice passes through *blood*, you are seeing, by means never explained. So enchanted noble fancy people flit around on flying tree sticks chasing creepy sentient orb and plotting fate of freaking world, because rest of us are not smart enough to take care of ourselves. Sure, this is thoroughly revolting way to organize society, if you are asking me, but if Brits and runny-nose American idiots want to lie around in warm puddle of Earl Grey tea dreaming of hobbits and Hogwarts, I will not stand on their way. But where we are coming from is not Hogwarts we're talking about. This is real thing, American-style. No whimsical wimple-wompers. No golden ticket. Reality at our school is random drug checks and security at the perimeters. *Shoot-on-sight* security."

"Are you finished?" said the driver. *Lester*, Beatrice said to herself. She'd heard someone call him Lester. Was anyone really called Lester anymore?

"*Nyet*. I am not finished. I have much more to say on subject of Harry Potter, Magical Capitalist Wizarding Boy."

From the back: "And everything else, for that matter."

"Anyway," said Lester, "we weren't exactly in school anymore. We were like, in *suspension*. Permanent D-Hall. For screw-ups. I'm Lester, by the way."

From somewhere out on Highway 146, a half-mile to the east, came the sound of a siren. The kids in the van were silent until the sound receded. *They're listening,*

Beatrice realized. *They're scared of being caught.* Maybe they were telling the truth after all. She took a step back from the vehicle.

"It's not screwed up to want to leave that place," said a different voice from the back. The girl this time. Beatrice could barely see her. She was sitting on the floor in the rear of the van, surrounded by what looked like vacuum cleaner parts and several large rotors. Her face was silhouetted by a bank of tiny orange LED lights. Her bubble gum popped like a tiny pistol.

"What was wrong with it?" asked Beatrice.

"It was evil," said the girl.

"It was worse than evil," said Mila. "It was boring."

"What's the difference?"

"We don't know what was wrong with it. We weren't allowed to know what was wrong with it. But we knew anyway."

"Shut your mouth, Lester."

"Look," said Lester, turning toward Beatrice again. "We can't really talk right now. Can you help us?"

"Help you how?"

"We're in big trouble. We need to get out of sight. Like, soon."

"You're pretty much out of sight now."

"Not from the street," said Lester, craning his neck to peer through the windshield. "From up there."

"Wait a second," said Beatrice. She took another step backward and squinted at the stars. "You're worried about *satellites*? Or what. *Drones*?"

"Dammit, Lester," said the girl in the back. "Let's go. It's too dangerous.

"She looks okay," said Lester.

"Not for us, dumbass," said the girl. She popped another bubble as if to punctuate her warning. "For *her.*"

The siren again. This time it was closer.

Three: The Kids in the Van

Beatrice had deeply, unapologetically red hair, like her grandmother, who always claimed it was as red as the blood of the fallen of Eire, "Eire" being an Irish word for, well, Ireland, which Beatrice's grandmother Clare could use because she actually was Irish but others obviously couldn't because they weren't. It was some kind of law. Also, Beatrice's face was galactically freckled, which didn't seem to be related to anyone's fallen and which her grandmother generally chose to ignore, even though it was also an Irish trait.

She—Beatrice, not her grandmother—stood five foot four in her basketball shoes and she probably wasn't going to get much taller, which hurt. Beatrice had always hoped she'd grow up lanky and languorous and possibly able to dunk. This was no longer likely. To her horror, she'd thickened up. She didn't feel like she was particularly aggressive or strong, but she was aware that other girls didn't like running into her and that she'd never been hurt, in practice or a game. In this general sturdiness she was like her father, a beer keg-shaped individual who could lift and carry a gas-powered generator and who approached life like a hungry man walking into a Luby's. And like her father, deceased but still adored, Beatrice was strong-willed, unimpressed by authority, and generous to a fault. Anyone who knew her could have predicted what happened next. That's how five strangers—five scruffy, *teenaged* strangers—ended up sitting in the living room of Beatrice's cramped duplex.

Fortunately for all concerned, Beatrice's mom was out for the evening. The exact reason, if you have to know, is that Frankie had teen court, as a result of an unfortunate incident at school involving the impulsive theft and felonious scarfing of a box of donuts intended for the Junior Honor Society. He planned to plead Not Guilty on account of extreme deliciousness. Anne and Frankie wouldn't be home till nine o'clock, which meant Beatrice had the place to herself. So she invited them in. At least she could finally get a good look at them. It was a seedy bunch. Marginal social skills. Hair in inappropriate places. At least three stick 'n poke tattoos. She realized they'd been telling the truth about being on the road. It was clear none of the group had showered for some time. She heard joints crackling as they arranged themselves on the couch and carpet.

There were three males and two females. The driver's name was Lester. *Lester White Bull*, he'd said, by way of introduction. He was a broken branch of a boy, with slender arms and wrists and an artist's gentle neck. He was wearing old blue jeans over a pair of brown boots, a faded army paratrooper's jacket and a black t-shirt. But that wasn't what Beatrice was thinking about at the moment. She was thinking about the blue-haired girl, Mila, who had just lit another Newport and was busy sucking down a mouthful of carcinogens. Nicotine. Formaldehyde. Hydrogen cyanide. For someone who was so obviously pleased with her own IQ, Mila seemed to lack a certain amount of common sense.

"Excuse me," said Beatrice.

"Hmm?"

"Do you mind?"

Mila glanced up at her. "Do I mind what?"

"Not smoking, please."

"Yes, I am minding. I need cigarette. Is this problem?"

"Could you go outside?"

"What? Like dog?"

"No. Not like a dog. Like a person who's smoking."

"You said mother and brother are not here. So sorry if I am causing problem for beautiful suburban home property."

"Excuse me? What's wrong with—?"

Lester chimed in. "I agree, man. That stuff is nasty. It's bad enough in the van, with the windows down…"

"Yeah," said the African-American girl who was sitting in the lounge chair. "Take it outside, Mila." She'd introduced herself to Beatrice as Chantel. She was tall and stout, with even features, high brows, and thick box braids framing a large forehead. Her fingernails were clipped short but painted bright orange, and Beatrice was momentarily distracted by the tattoo on the inside of Chantel's left arm. It said: PARANOID ANDROID.

"You're weak," said Mila. "All of you."

She stood up abruptly and walked out the door. Only a moment after she'd slammed it, she opened the door again and stuck her head in.

"You are keeping pie hole shut," she added, focusing on Lester.

But Lester's pie hole was wide open. He was demolishing the microwave popcorn Beatrice had just made. Two of the other kids—Chantel, who was wearing a MORDOR FUN RUN t-shirt with blue jeans and scarlet sneakers, and the tall East Indian kid named Sanjay, garbed in a long white garment that was either a lab coat or a nightgown—were helping him do it.

Only the Asian boy, Victor Cho, declined to eat. He wore beat-up running shoes, khaki shorts, a white undershirt, and a black leather jacket with a profusion of pockets. He was studying his laptop. Periodically his face scrunched up in an expression of dismay, or his eyelids inched upward to indicate surprise or pleasure, but otherwise he was still. It was an odd sight. It was if someone had a remote control for his face, and was practicing moving the features around. So far, Victor hadn't said a word, though he occasionally mumbled as his fingers flew around on his keyboard.

"So," said Beatrice, wincing as the cliché came out of her mouth. Cliches tasted a little like terrycloth, she remembered. But she couldn't help it. "Where are y'all from?"

The silence was deafening.

"Nowhere!" said Mila, from outside.

"Washington," said Lester. "The state."

"That's what she said," said Chantel.

"OK. So you live in Washington State."

"We were in *school* there. We weren't really living."

"And now you're here."

Victor Cho finally looked up from his laptop. He glanced around the room. "Evidently," he mumbled.

"Doing…?"

"What?"

"No. That's my question. Why are you here…like, in Texas?"

Beatrice's guests eyed each other warily.

"We're looking for someone," said Lester. "Someone in Austin. We think."

"You're a long way from Austin. That's like, four hours from here. Maybe five, with traffic."

"Yeah, *Lester.*"

Sanjay scoffed. "Lester said Houston was the next city over. Like, it was just next door."

"We need to get to Austin," Lester confirmed.

"You know, you guys don't have to tell me anything. If it's like, too weird. I was just asking."

"That's okay. We think they lost track of us somewhere in Idaho."

Sanjay nodded. "We took out our trackers."

"Trackers?"

"Micro-transmitters. Implanted just beneath the skin of our upper backs. Positioned so we couldn't get at them ourselves. We had to help each other. It got a little messy."

Beatrice rubbed her eyes. "Okay, so that's not really what I meant by *why*. What I really meant was, why is someone tracking you in the first place? With, you know…*micro-transmitters*?"

"Big brains," said Sanjay.

"Big brains?"

"Massive," Sanjay affirmed. "We have them."

"Yeah, no. Still not following."

Lester sat back with another handful of popcorn. "Look, our school is secret, okay? It's supposed to be this big governmental honors academy, but it's also classified."

"Never heard of it."

"That's what I'm saying. *No one's* ever heard of it. It's a highly confidential operation for education of what Lucas Todd—he's the jerk who runs the place—calls the best and the brightest."

"That's what he calls us. He doesn't know what we call him."

"He's like, the headmaster? Lucas Todd?"

"Head monster," said Chantel. "Tall, pale, and handsome. Sealed up tight as a Japanese watch."

"You know *The Wizard of Oz*?" Sanjay burst in. "He's like the Tin Man in a really nice cardigan. Let's try not to say his name for a while."

Lester set down his Sprite. "I'm okay with that. The Academy's all about STEM stuff. Science, Technology, Engineering, and Math. Which, in our case, means mostly robotics, fiber optics, nanotech and genetic engineering."

"Still never heard of it."

"No football team," grunted Mila, leaning in through the open front door. "That is your problem. No cheering team doing stints at halfway time."

"Though we do play quidditch," said Sanjay.

"Did play quidditch," said Chantel.

"Naked quidditch," said Sanjay, winking at Beatrice.

"Shut *up,*" groaned Chantel, squeezing her eyes shut. "I'm trying to eat here."

"But some of us got, like…what do you call it? Broom burn."

Victor Cho cackled, though it was unclear whether he was reacting to Sanjay's comment or something on the screen of his laptop.

Lester shook his head. "All right, four-year-olds. Can we concentrate for like, thirty seconds, please? Jesus. So…yes. We were at the Academy. And everything was great. Until we got sidetracked."

"Sidetracked."

"Diverted."

"Used and abused," said Chantel. She found the button to tilt her chair back and reclined until she was almost lying down. She smiled, then pushed the button to return upright. "That's what I'd call it."

"Those of us without a family," Sanjay added. "Without connections. With…who *need* things."

"I get it," said Beatrice. "You're like the X-Men."

"Right. Only we're all Professor X."

"Speak for yourself, nerd."

"Except for you. You're more like that Toad dude."

"Shut up."

"So you won't help us?" said Lester. His voice was as thin as a new moon's first sliver.

"I can like, give you *food*, I guess. More food, I mean. We have some diet Cokes."

"Got any weed?" said Sanjay.

Beatrice frowned. "Seriously?"

Chantel threw a wadded-up napkin at him. "Great plan, Sanjay. Let's run away from the feds and take our lives in our hands and then just stop in Texas so we can all get *baked*. You're a genius."

"Hey, I was just asking." Sanjay focused on Beatrice again. He was tall, with a mane of lustrous black hair and a facial furze the same color. His eyes were warm and dark, like chocolate left in the sun, and now they were trained on her and they didn't seem to be going anywhere in the near future. Sanjay ventured a midnight grin, mischievous and knowing, and Beatrice realized he thought he was a *player*. God's Pan-Asian gift to suburban white girls, maybe. And okay, she'd admit it, he was attractive enough, in a loungy, bootleg-video sort of way, but he wasn't her type. She wasn't crazy about confidence. She tended to like the whole visible rib cage, sweaters-and-glasses kind of boy, dreamy and prophetic, head buried in a book, hair tousled and insane. No, the Sanjay thing wasn't going to work. Sanjay's smile faded. Which was okay. She probably wasn't *his* type, either, but some boys had to try anyway. It was a dog-in-the-manger kind of deal, she figured.

"You're supposed to be special, right?" Sanjay continued. "I was thinking maybe you had some weed around to…you know. *Decompress.*"

Beatrice glanced around the room, which was suddenly silent. All eyes were on her.

"Special how?" She felt queasy all of a sudden. She realized this random meeting with a bunch of unknown runaways might not have been very random at all.

"You tell us," said Chantel. There didn't seem to be any pretense to Chantel. She was blunt and imposing, less a tree by the river than a boulder in the middle. She'd brought a yellow plastic bin of bolts, screws, and springs in from the van. Now, having eaten her fill of popcorn and tortilla chips, she started sorting the hardware. "Lester has a folder on you that's like, three inches thick. I've seen the damn thing. He says you can dream things so strong they really happen. You know anything about that?"

Beatrice tried to laugh. But she could feel the blood rush to her face, a reaction that was equal parts embarrassment and indignation. She wanted to deny it all, of course. She wanted to be angry, like an animal when it realizes it's walked into a trap. But she couldn't help it. Among the mix of sensations she was feeling was an undeniable sense of relief. It was as if she'd been recognized, finally, after a long period of hiding.

"Some kind of mess about a *dragon*," persisted the African-American girl. "Two or three years ago. Like, a mass hallucination of some sort—but one that was linked directly to you. There was speculation. Some dude wrote a paper about it." Chantel popped a bubble. "That it was like, *real*. Or that, if it wasn't, your mind was capable of some pretty freaky things."

"I don't know what you're talking about."

"No," said Mila, opening the door and leaning in again. "We didn't think so. Also others have written papers proving nothing happened at all and you are big Texas-type fraud maker."

"Lester's been on this kick for a long time," said Chantel. "And he was the one who brought us here. We were trying to get to Austin. Like I said, he was going on about how Houston was just the next town over. Like, we could *skate* over, right? Did I say that already?"

"Texas is a big place."

"Yeah," said Sanjay. "Big and ugly."

Beatrice stifled a pang of annoyance. She wasn't sure why, but she felt the need to defend her home state. All Texans do. "Said the person who lives in a van."

"Ooh," said Chantel. "Shots fired."

Victor Cho giggled, and Sanjay gave him an elbow in retaliation. Mila ambled back into the house and stood with her arms across her chest. "This was mistake, Lester White Bull. Redhead girl is no more help than you losing wallet in Casper, Wyoming. We are needing to be leaving this place. While we still can."

"I'm sorry," said Beatrice. "I don't know what to do for you."

"I do," said Lester. He and Chantel exchanged glances. "Come *with* us."

Beatrice glanced around the room. She wanted to treat the statement as a joke. Unfortunately, no one was laughing. "Wait, what? I can't—. There's no room, for one thing. It looks like someone took a car apart in the back of that van."

"There's room," said Chantel. "And it wasn't a car."

"Okay, but even so. I can't just go *with* you."

"Why not?" asked Sanjay. "Don't tell me you're worried about school. Are you going to miss nap time?"

"Well, there's that. School, I mean. I have a Spanish quiz tomorrow. And basketball practice, though that's not till Friday. But it's not *just* that. I mean, I don't even know you. Any of you. And my mom's not here."

Beatrice tried to ignore Mila's snort of derision.

"There is no room for Mom," she said. "And we will not be responsible for warming of baby bottle."

Lester peered at her through his curtain of hair. "You can sense things, can't you?"

Beatrice winced. "Sense things?"

"You know what I mean. Do you think we're dangerous?"

"A little. Maybe."

"Do you think you can trust us?"

"I can't tell."

"This is ludicrous! She is just standard-issuing American airhead."

"Shut up, Mila."

"Look," said Lester. "I think you could help us. I know why you don't want to talk about yourself. I would be the same way. But we know about the dragon. The basilisk."

"It wasn't a BASILISK!" snapped Mila, in what sounded like the continuation of an old argument. "You are mixing up your nonsense creatures."

"Whatever," said Lester. "We know it was associated somehow with your mental capacities—that it was a projection, or possibly a creation, of your mind. That's not like, *normal*. That means you're one of us. And if you have any sort of intuition or ability to sense things that other people can't, we need you."

"Because?"

Lester shrugged. His eyes drifted sideways to allude to his companions. Victor Cho was typing away at his laptop. Chantel was disassembling some complicated collection of springs and gaskets, snapping her gum. Mila still stood in the middle of the room, glaring at its inhabitants, only now she was biting her nails. And Sanjay was gazing into a make-up mirror, smoothing his beginner's moustache.

"We need an actual person. Someone who's okay with the world. We've been cooped up so long at the Academy, we don't know what we're doing out here. We don't know who to trust."

Beatrice nodded.

"I get it," she said. "And I'd like to help. But the answer is still no."

"Guys," said Victor. He stopped typing. His voice was so soft that all conversation instantly stopped. "We gotta go."

"Why?"

"Doomsday," he said, glancing up from his computer screen. "They've moved it up. People are going to start dying, like…"

"Like when?"

"Like, *soon.*"

High above Belgrove Avenue, the Northrop Grumman MQ-8 Fire Scout, an unmanned helicopter, processed the infrared images it was taking of the little duplex below. The murky video showed five figures inside the structure and one at the door. The footage was transmitted via radio to a CIA receiving station outside of Las Vegas, Nevada. And from there a message was delivered to an anonymous internet address in Washington State. A burly blonde man stood up from his desk and walked down the hall. He poked his head into the headmaster's office.

"Target acquired," he said.

Four: Anne's Boyfriend

Here's the thing about this guy Beatrice's mom was dating: He wasn't a fireman.

Before we proceed, the authors would like to make something clear. THERE IS NOTHING WRONG WITH NOT BEING A FIREMAN. Plenty of men aren't. In fact, most men aren't, and they get along fine. They sell homeowner's insurance, and fix power lines, and participate in commercial arbitrations. But let's face it. There's something loveable about a dude who dedicates his life to preparing for the day when he's called upon to rescue folks from a FIERY FREAKING DISASTER. It's nice to rescue people from accounting disasters. Plumbing mishaps can be unpleasant as well—especially at holidays! But still. They're not quite the same kinds of disasters as actual *gas lines exploding and timbers falling in fire-breathing houses that innocent people like you and me and possibly a golden retriever named Finley are struggling to get out of* types of disasters.

So, unlike Beatrice's late father, Larry Bartkowski was not a fireman. As far as Beatrice could tell, he wasn't especially adventurous, either—unless of course you count online dating as adventurous, which is how he met Anne. Larry was thirty-six, two years younger than Anne.

He was gainfully employed and humorless and helpful almost all the time.

Now it's true that sometimes he had to think about whether he was going to be helpful, as if being helpful were on a to-do list he'd saved in his head. And afterwards he was careful to make sure everyone *knew* he had helped, which of course further erodes the karmic prestige associated with true helpfulness. *Whatever.* He did help, and not everyone is St. Theresa and all.

Larry claimed he was a former FBI agent who now worked in cyber-security for an aerospace company that he wasn't supposed to talk about. Beatrice wasn't quite sure what working in "cyber-security" meant, but then again she didn't particularly care, either, since she was mainly interested in shooting three pointers and singing like Beyoncé and maybe, just maybe, attracting the attention of a slender blonde kid in her Geometry class named Cooper Litvic. Cooper wore cowboy boots and a Future Farmers of America jacket, but he also had a thing for reading battered old fantasy paperbacks, and he spent a lot of time gazing out the window of their classroom at the cars rushing by on Bay Area Boulevard as if they were his own scattered thoughts. Beatrice imagined he might grow up to be America's first really awkward country-western star, if he ever got that acne under control and learned to look people in the eye.

Cooper hadn't given Beatrice any indications that her crush was mutual. So far, she hadn't met a boy who did. Her heart was like that shop in the mall—the portrait studio, maybe, or the old people's shoe store—

that no one ever went in to. She was the last thing on the menu. She was the toy in the back of the closet. She could go on like this indefinitely. In fact, sometimes she did. And sometimes Bea figured maybe the reason she was so freaked out by her mom having a guy in her life was that she didn't have anyone interesting in hers.

Larry Bartkowski wasn't great. He wasn't terrible. He was just...*Larry*. He was like the original flavor at Pinkberry. He was tall and fit and somewhat vain—Beatrice had caught him more than once flexing for the mirror in the front hallway—and he rarely cracked a smile around Beatrice or Frankie. He had big hands with a lot of dark hair on them, like if they were separated from his arms they would just run off into the forest and live on their own, and the kind of skin that looked like it was stretched a little too tight over the bones of his face. He wasn't a light-hearted man. In fact, if you were quick enough, you could see him frowning at times when he thought no one was looking.

Again, *whatever.*

As long as her mother was happy, Beatrice was willing to give the guy a chance. She was polite when she needed to be, and just stayed away from him when she felt tempted to say something unkind. Larry bought her a basketball and came to a couple of her games, and he told her she'd played well when in fact she'd played pretty poorly. But mostly he knew better than to try to be her dad. As long as he kept his distance, and was kind to her mother, Beatrice kept her thoughts locked inside. They occasionally tried to get out. They rattled the doorknob and scratched at the windows, but for the most part they behaved themselves. They kept their voices down, and everyone was more or less happy. Or at least not all that unhappy.

And that's what life was all about, right?

Sometimes she thought to herself, that's what I'm going to put on my tombstone:

BEATRICE ANNE MCILVAINE
It Could Have Been Worse.

Five: The Dream

Beatrice dreamt that night.

Not about the dragon. That particular nightmare had never come back, praise the saints. As she recovered from the pain and fatigue of that extended psychological torment, her head cleared like a misty field in the morning sun. She'd never been bothered by visions of the creature again. And this was still true, because the vision that came to her this time was different. This was a dream of dread and menace, but she couldn't tell what was causing it. There was no particular person or object to fear. And yet the dread was there nonetheless. It was faint but hard to ignore, like a cell phone vibrating under a pile of clothes. In her head she searched underneath couch cushions, behind back seats, through the pockets of her jeans.

Nothing.

She didn't know what she was looking for, but she needed to find it. In fact, her inability to classify what she was looking for seemed to make locating it all the more urgent. In the sky to the west the clouds were freighted with a darkness deeper than rain. In her mind she saw storms churning an icy sea, waves so high they hid the heavens, winds ripping trees out of the earth in some wild range of North Country forest. And all the while the noise persisted: first a humming, but gradually growing in volume and intensity. There was something very wrong happening near her and the noise was getting louder. It was vacuuming, maybe. That was it. A giant troll—vacuuming. Or hammering. Jackhammering. No. Even louder. The walls of her room shook. Beatrice rolled out of bed and sat facing the door. She wasn't sure if she was awake or still dreaming, but she knew she was scared. The clock by her bed said 3:09. *Does anything good ever happen*, she asked herself, *at three o'clock in the morning?* Beatrice heard voices in the hallway. She turned her head back to the door just in time to watch as it was blown off its hinges into her bedroom.

The beams of several flashlights bounced around the room.

"CLEAR!" someone shouted.

Men in black combat gear—helmets, goggles, body armor—crowded around her.

"Beatrice MCILVAINE!" said a voice. "Put your hands where I can see them. You're coming with us."

She screamed for as long as she could. She kicked and punched and tried to make it through the wall of bodies to the door, but someone heaved her back onto the bed and put a knee on her chest. She felt cold fingers on her skin. She felt like her sternum was about to snap. She couldn't breathe. Then she was aware of the single sharp prick of a needle in the soft flesh of her neck, and the world started floating away.

She could hear voices. Men's voices, mostly. But also her mother's, sounding increasingly frantic. Once she thought she heard Frankie calling to her from a very great distance. But mostly she heard the men hollering to each other, and then the *whump-whump-whump* of the helicopter that had set down in the field behind her house. *So that's what the noise was*, she told herself. Not a dragon. Not exactly, at least. A dragon machine. A drag*onfly*. She wanted to call out again but she couldn't. All she could do was close her eyes. Finally the voices went away and the noises and the sound of her own thoughts. She slept, and this time there were no dreams. The black lands of unconsciousness stretched out around her, pitiless and empty, and she stopped being afraid. In fact, for the moment, she stopped being anything at all.

Six: Suspicions

Oh, and another thing about Larry Bartkowski. Sometimes—and, okay, this isn't like an established fact, mind you, so keep that in mind—but sometimes, Beatrice would come back from school and look over her things and swear to herself, not knowing it but *feeling* it, that someone had been in her room. Handling her books. Pawing through her journals. Checking her browsing history on the old laptop she kept on her desk.

Could she prove it?

No.

Did she know it?

Yes.

Seven: Taken

"Ah," said a voice. The tone was deep and clear. Soothing somehow. It might have been the voice of a DJ on a classical music station—one of those old dudes who sounds like he's speaking in fluent cappuccino.

Or a life coach—if your life mostly involves taking care of office plants.

Or possibly a con man.

Beatrice opened her eyes.

"Waking up, I see."

"Oh my God," she said. "Where am I?"

She was sitting in a brightly lit conference room. A man she'd never seen before was sitting across a glass table from her. Another man occupied a chair by the door.

"Good morning, Beatrice. You're in the Pacific Northwest. Washington State, actually. And you're perfectly safe."

"Great. But... Wow. I can't talk."

"I understand your family calls you Bea. Is that right?"

"It is."

"Can I call you Bea?"

"No."

"Okay, I get it. You're skeptical. That's cool. You're waking up from a little sedative we gave you last night. You might want to take it easy for a few minutes. You may be dizzy for a while."

"I feel like I'm…"

"You feel like you're waking up at the bottom of a well, right?"

"Something like that."

The man gave her a sympathetic smile as he pushed a plastic water bottle across the table toward her. "Beatrice, it's a pleasure to meet you. My name is Lucas Todd. You don't know me, but I've been aware of you for quite some time. You drink coffee? We can get you some if you'd like. Or kava, maybe?"

Beatrice rubbed her eyes. She felt as if she'd been asleep for a week.

"Aware of me? I'm not sure what that means, but it sounds inappropriate." She gazed around the room again. There were no windows. She had no clue where she was, and hadn't the foggiest notion of the time. She wasn't even sure what day it was. She yawned. "What's kava?"

The man sitting across from her was middle-aged, well-groomed, obviously fit. He had a full head of silver hair, neatly trimmed, and a pair of expensive glasses with clear frames that accented his tanned face. It was a big face, too—larger than normal, compared to the rest of his body. His eyes were green, and he had a habit of fixing them on his subject, lizard-like and unblinking, as he spoke. He nodded as if he'd expected Beatrice's questions, and planned to deal with them in due time—as if they were trivialities; details; dots to be connected for a slow and stubborn child.

"Again, you're safe. Let's start there. There's nothing sketchy going on. You're in a United States government facility at a location I'm not at liberty to disclose any more precisely than I already have. And kava's a drink. Very soothing. Some people call it nature's Xanax. It's made from the roots of plants native to the South Pacific, but we grow our own, and frankly it's an improvement on the original."

"Umm. Maybe not. What's that?"

Beatrice's questioner was drinking from what looked like a stainless-steel cylinder.

"Water," he answered. "Triple-filtered."

"Two filters aren't enough?"

"It's no fault of yours, Beatrice. I want you to understand that first of all."

"*What's* not a fault of mine? Why am I here? Where's my mom? She's gonna freak out if she doesn't know where I am. And trust me, you do not want to see my mom freak out. It's like an earthquake happens in her head. I need my phone. I have *streaks*, for God's sake. I'm at 404 days with Jennifer."

"Streaks."

"On Snap. You—never mind. It's stupid."

"You'll get your phone back eventually. In the meantime, trust me. Your mother is safe. Your little brother is safe. Frankie? Is that his name? He's a pistol, that kid. Fought like a champ. He thought we were trying to hurt you, I guess. Nothing could be further from the truth. Please don't panic."

"I'm not panicking. I just…what?"

"Your heart rate is spiking. Your pupils are dilated. I'm a physician, Beatrice. I can tell when someone is starting to panic."

"Look, I just don't understand what's going on. Why am I here? And how did I get here?"

"You were recently contacted by a very dangerous group of terrorists."

Beatrice's head snapped back. "*Terrorists?* What are you talking about?"

"Your mother's been informed that you've been detained for questioning, and—"

"You're talking about those freaks in the van? I don't even know those kids."

"That's odd. They spent time in your house."

"How did you know that?"

"We know lots of things, Beatrice. And not just about our little group of runaways. We know a few things about you as well. Not so long ago, there were people at our institution who thought you had abilities— *abnormalities*, might be the better term—that could be useful to us. To the government."

Beatrice squeezed her eyes tight. She slapped her forehead with her open palm. "Oh my God. Not this again. If you mean I have weird dreams, okay. I admit it. I've been to counseling for that. I went to the…you know. The *clinic*. They tested me. They took like, a gallon of blood. They made me get in one of those big metal tubes for an MRI. Then they made Frankie take tests. It was totally stupid and ridiculous and I don't know how to explain it now any better than I did back then. But I don't know why you would care about that. Or how it's any of your business."

"That's because you don't know my business. And surely you realize not all people's dreams about giant dragons actually seem to become *giant dragons*, visible to witnesses on the ground?"

Beatrice glanced up. The man across the table was smiling again. She felt a drop of sweat start to crawl down her back.

"I'll take that coffee," she said.

"We're especially interested in the leader of the cell that contacted you."

"Lester?" She wasn't sure how she knew the skinny kid with the doomed goatee was the leader, but she did.

"Lester White Bull. Indeed. Born of an Oglala Lakota woman on the Pine Ridge Reservation on July 9th, 2003. Mom died giving birth. Dad was a cable repairman. He didn't want the baby, and Lester was put up for adoption when he was just a few months old. Kid spent his first six years in a series of foster homes. Showed advanced mathematical abilities by the age of five. We brought him to our facility on his ninth birthday."

"Let me guess," said Beatrice. "You sent an owl."

"Good one. But no. We sent a Tahoe."

"I don't think he liked it there. Here. Wherever we are."

Lucas Todd frowned. "Oh, he liked it fine at first. It was a step up for him. Several steps up, as a matter of fact. But he's a rebellious young man. Sullen. If he were on the reservation, he'd be dead by now. Alcohol. Opiates. That's what his psych profile indicates, anyway."

Beatrice took another sip of coffee. It was weak, and too sweet, but she drank it anyway. She needed to focus.

"I still don't understand. What does Lester White Bull have to do with me?"

"We had Lester analyzing data related to your dragon ideation. He asked for information about you, and we supplied it. Photos. Social media feeds. Interviews with neighbors and school officials. We eventually figured out the dragon-in-the-sky episode was a sort of mass hallucination. One person thought he saw something. He reported it. Someone else joined in. Sort of like the chupacabra phenomenon a few years back. A whole slew of sightings was eventually traced to a single call to a late-night radio show. Even Lester eventually agreed with the conclusion. But by then he was spending more time looking at your Instagram page than doing any actual work."

"My Insta—? Okay, that's enough. He's not even on my feed."

"Not officially, no."

"Jesus. You mean he was spying on me? I want to go home. Get me a lawyer or something. You guys are creeping me out."

Lucas Todd shrugged. "We'll get you home. We just need a little help first."

"Help with what?"

Lucas Todd glanced sideward at the man who was sitting beside the door. For the first time, the man looked up. He was older, closer to sixty, perhaps, but now, as he straightened in his chair, Beatrice could see that he was tall and powerfully built. He was clearly no one to trifle with, despite his age. She had the odd sensation that she hadn't paid any attention to him before because he hadn't wanted her to. It was almost as if he'd been hiding in plain sight. He had blue eyes, olive-tinted skin, and long dark hair flecked with gray. Unlike Todd, he was casually dressed. He wore jeans and a white linen shirt open at the neck to reveal several necklaces. He frowned at Beatrice, scratched his dark beard, and nodded. If he was trying to communicate something, either to her or to Todd, Beatrice couldn't tell what it was. But the man didn't seem to care. He stood and walked out of the room. Slowly, at the pace a bear might move.

Okay, thought Beatrice. *That was weird.*

Todd spoke again. "What did they tell you, Beatrice?"

"Who? The kids in the van?"

"The kids. Yes."

"Not much. I don't even remember some of their names."

Todd sat back in his chair, exhaling heavily. "Is that so? Let me refresh your recollection." He reached for a remote the size of a matchbook and swiveled in his chair to face the wall at the back of the room. He pointed the remote at the ceiling and the lights dimmed. Then he pointed it at the wall and images appeared. The first was a photograph of the blue-haired girl who'd been riding shotgun with Lester.

"Ludmila Konradi," he said. "They call her Mila. Age 17. IQ comparable to Lester's—which is to say, phenomenal. A talented linguist and cryptographer. She speaks six languages, which is ironic, given that her smoking habit is going to destroy her vocal cords in a few years. Depressive personality. Trouble with authority figures."

"Like you?"

"Especially me."

The next picture up was the Chinese boy who rarely spoke. Thick black hair. Lips so thin she could barely see them. A flat, suspicious gaze at the camera.

"Victor Cho. 15. Computer whiz. Hacker. Virtual reality aficionado. Definitely on the spectrum, though high-functioning. Once spent 43 hours penetrating Department of Defense security protocols. After he made it through, we thought he'd gone to bed. We found him two hours later playing *Call of Duty* on one of the mainframes. It's quite possible he doesn't know what a tree looks like. Taiwanese parents, both engineers.

They died in a car wreck on an LA freeway when he was four."

Next, the Indian boy. *Sanjay.* Standing in what looked like a garage in a white robe and a pair of maroon high-tops.

"Sanjay Rana. Gujarati. Communications and satellite expert. Narcissist and wannabe ladies' man. We found him on the Internet when he was running the streets of Rajkot, teaching people how to jailbreak their iPhones. He was seven. His mother died of ovarian cancer not long after we made contact, and we brought him here."

"Question."

"Yes?"

"Why does he wear that bathrobe?"

Lucas Todd studied the photograph for several seconds. "I couldn't tell you."

The final photograph was a shot of the African-American girl.

"And, finally, Chantel Griggs. Seventeen. Photographic memory. The engineer of the group. She was left on the doorstep of a Catholic church in Detroit when she was six weeks old. In the middle of a blizzard. She jerry-rigged that van to run on garbage. That's why we haven't been able to track these guys by fuel purchases. All they need is a load of bio-mass and they're good for another two hundred miles. That's our bunch of runaways. Talented but disturbed. Very talented, in fact. And very disturbed. We need them back."

The image faded.

"They're not terrorists," said Beatrice. "They're teenagers."

Lucas Todd shrugged. "They're not terrorists in the traditional sense, no. They're not religious fanatics. They're not political. Not yet, anyway. But trust me. They're dangerous."

"Why?"

"Why what?"

"Why do they need to be here?"

"Because they have nowhere else to go. And their work is important."

"What work is that?"

Todd chuckled mirthlessly. Beatrice wondered if his face betrayed a brief flash of impatience. "I'm afraid that's not something I can discuss with you."

"Why not? Too many big words?"

"Suffice it to say, it's classified. And it's almost complete."

"Lester was convinced it was something bad."

"Lester has an over-active imagination. The work we're doing here is good, important stuff. It's something he'll be proud of one day. Unfortunately, Mr. White Bull exhibits many of the symptoms of post-traumatic stress disorder. Especially the paranoia. He and a couple of the other kids became convinced they were engaged in something nefarious. That we were using them, somehow, for bad ends. I assure you this isn't true. Lester and his friends were always treated well here, and we want them back. In fact, we need them back, if only for long enough to make sure they haven't run off with materials or information they're not supposed to have. Make no mistake. Lester White Bull is an unstable individual."

"He seemed okay to me."

"I'm sure he was on his best behavior. He wants you involved."

"He does? Why?"

Todd considered her closely. His green eyes narrowed.

"Come with me," he said. "And I'll show you."

The campus of the Academy sprawled over several hundred acres high on an eastern slope of Washington's Cascade Mountains. Douglas firs towered like ancient American gods over crushed granite paths. A cold-water creek burbled clear as gin down a rocky course, and blue jays—bigger than the ones in Texas, and black-headed—cawed from the canopies of the trees. Lucas Todd paused in a patch of sun-stippled yellow and white wildflowers. They were asters, maybe, or daisies. Beatrice wasn't good with flowers. Her mother might know. She could snap a photo and text her mom and—. No. Delete. She couldn't—*because she didn't have her phone*. Its absence made her feel physically ill. Aside from eating and sleeping, she used it for just about everything. Socializing. Studying. *Avoiding* studying. As Beatrice watched, a hummingbird zipped past her ear. Or wait.

Not a hummingbird. A tiny mechanical device, with three propellers making a barely audible hum as the machine maneuvered through the trees.

At almost the same moment, Beatrice spotted another of the little flyers passing overhead. This one was the size of a fist.

"Beautiful, isn't it?" said Todd.

"I guess," she answered. "Except for the drones."

"Oh. Right. They can be a nuisance. But at least they're quieter now than they used to be. The kids can't get enough of 'em. They carry messages, deliver homework, help with experiments. You name it. But aside from that—what do you think of our little garden of the gods? Impressive, no?"

Beatrice nodded. It *was* impressive. It was like stepping ten years into the future. Maybe twenty.

"I called this place Hogwarts when I first talked to Lester. That didn't go over too well."

"You didn't say that to Mila, I hope."

"I did. Mistake. But I have to admit this is…better."

"The British claim to have magic, as I'm sure you know. Deep, ancestral magic of some sort, genetically encoded, that manifests itself in certain individuals around the time puberty sets in. We don't have that luxury, I'm afraid. Not puberty. We have plenty of that. I mean *magic*. All our 'wizardry' is the result of a little Yankee ingenuity and a whole lot of elbow grease. Like the lightbulb. And the Model T. And the first airplane. And the PC. And the iPhone. All American innovations, of course. We start with the basics. You'll recall that no one at Hogwarts ever seems to study algebra, or earth sciences, or even anything as fundamental as grammar or history. The end result is a bunch of purportedly enchanted individuals who are, in fact, mathematically illiterate. Not here. Our students are the best of the best. Truly gifted. They're the kind of people we want to engineer our future. But we make sure they get a thorough grounding in the academic basics before they move on to their true callings—astrophysics, or quantum theory, or biogenetics."

"Biogenetics?"

"Exactly."

"How could genetics be anything other than 'bio'?"

"Well, it could be *cyber*-genetics, which we're——Wait. Hold on. That's a clever question, young lady, but I'm afraid you don't have clearance to hear what's going on in that area. And the learning isn't just academic. It's practical. We grow our own food from modified seed stores. We brew our own kombucha here and—as I mentioned—cultivate a cold-climate version of kava. We manufacture and install our solar panel arrays. And all our buildings are modeled on Frank Lloyd Wright's notions of working with nature rather than against it. Notice the long, low lines. All the stone and wood— spruce and fir, mostly—and glass. The construction *into* the mountain rather than on top of it. No house should ever be on a hill, Beatrice, or indeed *on* anything. It should be *of* the hill. Belonging to it. Hill and house should live together, each the happier for the other. Forgive me if I sound like I'm preaching. I get a little excited about this place sometimes, partly because I helped to design it. In case you're wondering, we're about ninety percent solar here, with some auxiliary energy supplied by wind and a couple of other sources I can't talk about. We're completely off the grid—when we want to be. And we've got the electronic resources to make ourselves essentially disappear if need be."

Beatrice gazed through a gap in the trees, trying to figure out what a distant group of kids was doing. They stood in a loose circle around two smaller figures, clearly robots, that were dancing, or—no, that wasn't right. Not dancing. They were *fighting*. Beatrice could hear vague shouts of encouragement and scorn from the circle as one of the robots lifted the other off the ground and slammed its opponent to the turf.

"But it's not all hard work," said Todd, observing the action. "There's always time for some recreation."

"What kind of recreation is that?"

"That? That's a duel between two Digitally-Operated Battle Bots. DOBBies, for short. Quite popular these days. One of the best of them is named after me, I'm told. Are you into robotics?"

"Sorry, no," she said. "Basketball."

"Basketball. That's right."

'That's right'? thought Beatrice. *What does that mean?* After a few minutes of easy downhill walking, they reached a low-set building of brown stone and unfinished spruce near the foot of one of the campus's hills. Lucas Todd led the way inside. With Beatrice following, he proceeded down three flights of stairs and

into a maze of hallways lit with clusters of what Todd explained were light-emitting diodes. A low-pitched hum emanated from somewhere in the complex, as if the building were deep in contemplation. There wasn't a window in sight. Clearly they were underground. In fact, Beatrice suspected they were walking beneath the slope they'd descended just a few minutes earlier.

Beatrice heard it before she could see it: a scrabbling racket from around the corner, metallic and harsh. It sounded like a car with a backseat full of sauce pans being driven over several sets of railroad tracks. A few moments later, a four-legged mechanical nightmare, four feet tall, fashioned of rubber and bright blue aluminum, loped into view from around the corner. Two mirror-like eyes gleamed as the thing approached.

"Relax," said Todd. "Just one of our mobile sentries. Let it scan your face. Your features have already been uploaded to the system."

Beatrice stood as still as she could as the creature, a robot modeled vaguely on someone's notion of a dog, glanced from Lucas Todd to her. A red light flickered over her face. It took a little longer than was completely comfortable. Finally some signal was received in its neural processors and the creature seemed satisfied. Its mechanical tail wagged twice, and it trotted off down the hallway in search of new pedestrians to confront.

"You couldn't afford a real dog?" said Beatrice.

"Real is outdated. We're making upgrades."

"How is that an upgrade?"

But her guide didn't answer. They stopped outside a door marked 613. Todd placed his thumb on the security device on one side of the doorway and Beatrice heard the click of a lock.

Todd pushed the door open.

"Lester's room," he announced.

Beatrice stepped in and gazed around the little chamber. It was a modest accommodation, windowless, of course, and dominated by a large desk on the wall opposite the door. It had hardwood floors, a single bed, unmade, and a built-in dormitory-style refrigerator. But none of this registered at first. Bea heard herself gasp. Every wall of the room was covered with photographs of her. Her. Beatrice McIlvaine. *Driving for a lay-up against Clear Creek. Waiting for the bus with her bestie, Jennifer Ramos. Walking out of school in the afternoon, wincing in the walloping South Texas sun.*

"Oh my God," she whispered. "This is so wrong."

"Agreed. Lester has some pronounced obsessive-compulsive characteristics. We tried to help him with that, apparently without much effect. He obviously wanted you involved. He probably had that in mind from the moment he and his friends made their escape. So here you are. *Involved.*"

"I don't want to be involved. I swear to God, I barely know these kids."

"I believe you," said Todd. He leaned back against the wall and pulled out his phone. "But they know you. At least, Lester does. And now you're going to help us get them back."

"What's that supposed to mean?"

"It means Lester has contacted us. He's confirmed that he has something of ours that we need to have returned. And now we have something of his that he wants as well."

Beatrice closed her eyes.

"That's right," said Todd. "You."

"Okay, look. This is ridiculous. First of all, I'm not *his*. I don't care how many pictures he has. He doesn't own me. And it doesn't matter if he's tracking everything I post on social media. The fact is, we've met once. And he's not going to be like, willing to trade something important just to *see* me again."

"That's not how love works, Beatrice. You're a girl. Did you not know that?"

"Really?"

"Really what?"

"You said that? Seriously? This is all really interesting and all, but I've seen enough. I'm not helping you with whatever game you're trying to play. I just want to go home."

Beatrice was almost to the door when she heard the words. "Of course you do. Because you want to see your mother, right?'

She turned. "Yeah? So? Is that supposed to be weird or something?"

"And you love your mother. Yes?"

Beatrice felt queasy. She didn't like the way the conversation was going. Naturally she loved her mother. Who doesn't love her mother? But something prevented her from saying the words. She remembered a book she'd read for freshman English. *1984.* The world's most important novel, her teacher called it. It was written in 1948, and it was supposed to be about the future, even though the actual 1984 was long past by now. In the book, the government controlled people by finding out their worst fear. And that's what they threatened you with if you did something they didn't like. The main character was a man named Winston Smith. His biggest fear was rats. Never mind exactly how the government tortured poor old Winston Smith, but needless to say, it involved rats. Nasty, hungry, squirrel-sized rats. The experience was so terrifying and painful that Winston Smith turned against the one person he loved—possibly the one person in the world who was still *worthy* of love. Beatrice disliked rodents, to be sure. But her bigger fear was different, and more diffuse. She worried more about something bad happening to her family.

"What's your point?"

"So here's why I think you'll help us. Let me show you a video. It's a funny little piece. Not generally available. My sources tell me what you're about to see took place in Iraq, two years ago." Todd spoke into his watch. "Tom, do you copy?"

"Here, chief," said a tiny voice from the speaker in the watch.

"You're patched into Lester's machine?"

"Affirmative."

"Bring up the clip, if you please."

Beatrice glanced at the monitor on Lester's desk. It had the biggest screen she'd ever seen. A grainy clip of black-and-white video—surveillance footage, she guessed, from a security camera—started playing. In it, a uniformed soldier stood in a hallway with a machine gun slung over his shoulder. A digital time stamp flickered in the bottom left corner. Only a few seconds passed before the guard looked to his right, then stepped forward, as if trying to see something just beyond his field of vision. A moment later, another figure moved into the frame from the guard's left. This figure was dressed all in black. He approached the guard from behind, locked his left arm around the man's throat and seemed to punch him several times with his right hand. The guard slumped to the floor to reveal that his attacker held a knife, dark with blood. The killer glanced up at the camera. The clip froze at that moment, catching the assassin's features full on. Beatrice felt her stomach fall away inside her. She recognized the killer's face. It was Larry Bartkowski.

Several seconds passed. Lucas Todd examined his fingernails. He was a man holding all aces, and he knew it.

"All right," said Beatrice, swallowing hard. Just as she'd done a hundred times before, she shoved her rage down where it couldn't be seen. Where it couldn't hurt anybody. It wouldn't do any good to show it now. Things got ugly when Beatrice got mad. It was more than just a matter of painting cloud pictures in the sky. The wind broke windows. Sidewalks cracked. She wasn't proud of her abilities. In fact, she was scared of what her mind could do. And hurting someone here wasn't going to help anyone at home in Texas. The fact was, she was a prisoner. Coffee and campus tours aside, she was someplace she didn't know, far from home, and a cold-blooded killer was in a position to hurt her family before Beatrice could do anything about it. She glanced again at the frozen face on the video. At the assassin her mother thought she was in love with.

"Okay," Beatrice sighed. "I'll help. And one other thing."

"Yes?"

"You suck."

Eight: Anne's Vigil

Just about anything you can say about Anne McIlvaine's reaction to Beatrice being abducted in the middle of the night by goggle-wearing commandos and flown off in a black helicopter would be an understatement.

Confused? *Of course.*

Worried? *Doesn't cut it.*

Frantic? *Closer.*

Larry Bartkowski was trying to be helpful. She'd give him that. And though Anne was annoyed that the FBI agents who'd come to offer the Bureau's official explanation for the detention of her daughter seemed to talk mostly to Larry, rather than to her, she was grateful he was there. But the gratitude faded.

First of all—and this was admittedly irrational—Larry had been making her tea. This sounds fine, right? The tea seemed to calm her down. But that was the issue. She didn't *want* to be calm. This wasn't the *time* for calm. Her daughter had been taken in the middle of the night and no one was willing or able to tell her where she'd gone or how long she'd be there. And Larry's solution was herbal tea. She drank it and then she grew quiet, and Frankie stared at her, puzzled, and mostly what she wanted to do was sleep. Was it her imagination? And what about this? For some reason, Larry seemed to be more interested in supporting the official position—the *FBI's* position—than in finding out the things Anne cared about, like FOR THE LOVE OF GOD WHERE IS MY DAUGHTER AND WHEN WILL SHE BE BACK?

The official story was that Beatrice had been contacted—perhaps inadvertently, and through no fault of her own—by a group of dangerous terrorists. The nature and identity of the terrorists was left undisclosed, as a matter of national security. Anne's daughter had been detained for questioning. No, she didn't need a lawyer. No, there was no need to involve the press or the local police. And no, Anne couldn't talk to Beatrice—not yet—even by cell phone.

Anne checked her Life360 app a dozen times. She knew Beatrice wasn't still at home—home was just where she'd been the last time her phone had checked in via microwave with the Global Positioning Satellite System. But in an odd sort of way it was comforting to see her daughter's little wizard icon gazing up at her from their home address. It was like a promise of her return, an affirmation of normality. The FBI agents understood. They humored her. This was standard protocol, they said. Beatrice was being well taken care of, ma'am. She'd be home soon, safe and sound. In the meantime, Anne was encouraged to keep the situation quiet. There was no need for press coverage. She didn't even need to tell her friends. The matter would be resolved as quickly as possible.

"I hope they know what they're doing," said Anne, watching from the living room window as the two agents returned to their car.

"I'm sure they do," said Larry, easing himself down on the sofa to study the news on his phone. "I'll bet this happens more often than we hear about."

"I mean, I'm as patriotic as the next person. I want to fight terrorism too. But this is—this is beyond all that. I'll give it one more day. Then…"

"Then what?"

"I don't know. I just can't… What if she's *frightened*? What if she's hungry?"

Larry lifted his feet to rest them on the coffee table. "Well, according to the feds, she's not a suspect. She's just a witness. I would expect they're going to treat her very well. I've seen how these things work. They know she's a very special young lady."

Anne turned away from the window. Her complexion paled. "What's that supposed to mean?"

"What's what supposed to mean?"

"*Special.* Bea's spent a good part of her life the last couple of years trying *not* to be special. Trying to control her emotions. She is not a normal person, you know. Why do you even say that?"

Larry stood to face her.

"Wow," he said. "You are really stressed out. I just meant, special to us. To *you*. And of course I think she's special too. She's our little Bea, right?"

Frankie was watching from the hallway. He and his mother exchanged glances before Frank shook his head and turned away.

"Hey," said Larry. "Calm down. Can I make you some tea? Or, I don't know. Kava?"

Nine: Reunion

Dreams again.

And the dark.

Beatrice stood in a vast, empty room. She could hear herself calling, though she couldn't make out the words. There was a single small window in one wall of the room and she went to it and gazed outside. She saw empty houses. She saw cars cruising the streets, moving in no particular hurry, but no one was in them. And that was a problem. Because she was looking for someone. No one in particular—just someone she could talk to. But there wasn't a soul to be seen, and Beatrice felt as if she'd been tricked. It was as if a friend had promised to meet her and hadn't showed up. She was curious at first, and then worried. Finally she was angry. She felt a tide of rage welling up within her, black fury boiling at this betrayal. She was standing in a field now and clouds were swirling above her. She looked up and waited for a figure to form. Light flickered in the darkness, and she heard the distant mumble of thunder. She was sweating and her fists were clenched in hard little balls and the clouds moved faster, agitated, trying but unable to form themselves into a recognizable message or warning. And then someone was shaking her out of her dream and back into the world. She was relieved. Bad things were happening in her head and she was glad to be leaving.

The relief lasted until she realized where she was.

Beatrice woke up in the back seat of a large vehicle that was moving fast on a broad, hilly highway. She'd been drugged again. She was sick to her stomach, and her skull felt as if it had been rolled around in a cement mixer for an hour or two. She took a sip of cool water from the plastic bottle in the cup holder in front of her, closed her eyes, tried to find some sense of balance. This took a while. She might have slept some more. When she finally felt well enough to be curious, the car was no longer moving. She was sitting between two burly men in business suits. They both wore sunglasses against the glare from outside. Wherever they were, it was bright.

AUSTIN LOVES YOU SO MUCH, said a billboard.

Ah, she thought. *Back in Texas. That explains the sunlight.*

One of the men glanced at his phone.

"The tracking network's online," he announced.

Beatrice didn't have to be told who he was talking about. The vehicle eased forward a few feet, then stopped again, and Lucas Todd swiveled around in the passenger seat to look back at her. Outside the car, an amiable army of young people passed by. Some carried flags—American, Mexican, the skull and crossbones, a giant peace symbol—on long, flexible poles. A man in a top hat and mutton-chop sideburns, wearing black suspenders, walked by on stilts. Barefoot women in straw hats and cotton sundresses flocked together, showing off glitter tattoos and hennaed hands. Moms wheeled strollers, and dads carried toddlers on their shoulders. Beatrice felt a whole rainbow of responses. It started with joy, shaded to envy, and ended in anger. She was still wearing her ratty blue jean cut-offs from two nights before, along with an oversized, distinctly unflattering Clear Lake High School t-shirt and a pair of black Converse sneakers she'd been given at the Academy. She needed a bath. She was hungry and thirsty and she had a vicious headache.

She was starting to feel very alone. And a little scared.

Calm down, she told herself. It was one of the coping skills they'd taught her at the clinic she went to after the fight with the dragon. *Breathe. Everything will be fine.*

"I still have no idea what Lester and Mila told you," said Lucas Todd. "But I suspect you know they're in Austin looking for someone. This particular someone is not to be trusted. His name is Paul Geiger. He's a rogue agent of a foreign government who has attempted to sell secrets of the United States to the highest bidder. He's an extremely untrustworthy individual."

"Yeah? Sort of like your friend Larry Bartkowski?"

"You're not helping matters, Beatrice."

Beatrice tried to shake herself alert. "OK. Have it your way. So what's this dangerous man doing here? Is he supposed to be a terrorist too?"

"He's a music enthusiast, evidently. Or, not so much a music enthusiast in this case. A *Luddites* enthusiast. The real Luddites were anti-technology terrorists in 19th Century England. They were workers—skilled craftsmen, mostly—who went around destroying industrial machinery they thought was going to take away their jobs. They were right about that, by the way. It did take away their jobs. Technology generally triumphs in the end. But the Luddites we're talking about are just a British musical group. Tear-down-the-system socialist types."

"Actually, two of them are Irish," one of the security guys said. He was blonde and close-shaven, with the hint of a tattoo peeking out from the collar of his button-down shirt. "The band uses a lot of mandolin and older instruments, even a hurdy-gurdy on one of their songs. Some of it has a Zeppelin-like vibe to it. *Over the Hills and Far Away.* That kind of thing."

Lucas Todd stared at the man as if he'd just sneezed in his coffee. "Are you done? Yes? Okay, so they use a lot of *mandolin*, and maybe even a *hurdy-gurdy*, and two of them are *Irish*, for anyone who gives a rat's ass. Very popular a decade or two ago. Now on a comeback tour, including a stop in Austin for what's called... What's it called?"

"What's what called, chief?"

Todd gestured impatiently at the crowd that surrounded them. "All of *this*, you idiot. All of this stupidity and chaos and...people."

"ACL Fest," said the driver.

"ACL. Right. That's why the kids think he may be in the vicinity. The man they're looking for has been here at least two of the last three years, according to facial recognition technology, though he tries to disguise his appearance. The Luddites play tomorrow. And that's when we're going to trade your release for the return of Lester and his friends. We won't really be trading you, you understand. At the end of the day, we're going to have all of you back where you belong. For you, that means...whatever that little place was."

"Seabrook."

"Seabrook. Beautiful Seabrook. With your mother and your little brother. But for Lester and his friends, I'm afraid it's going to mean something a little less pleasant."

"So I'm the bait."

"You," Todd agreed, "are the bait."

"What makes you think this is going to work?"

"Oh, it'll work. You saw those photographs pinned to the walls in Lester's room. I sent Lester a note on the one subreddit I know he still checks. I told him I was willing to let you walk if he and his friends will get our stolen property back to us."

"Or...?"

"Or what?"

Beatrice's headache was starting to fade. She took another swallow of water. "There has to be more, right? What if he doesn't show up?"

"You're a clever girl, Beatrice. I happened to mention that if he *doesn't* show up, Beatrice McIlvaine will be spending the rest of her life in prison for aiding and abetting his theft from a federal facility."

Beatrice shook her head. She gazed up through the sunroof.

"Does the word 'scumbag' mean anything to you?"

"It's a bluff. But it's an effective bluff, I think. Lester is here. I can feel it. They're all here. And you can feel it too, can't you?"

"I don't have to feel it," she said.

"What's that supposed to mean?"

Beatrice met Lucas Todd's gaze and refused to blink. *This guy*, she thought, *is starting to get on my nerves.*

"Look out your window."

Lucas Todd craned his neck in the direction Beatrice was pointing. There was a message written high in the powder blue sky. A drone was just finishing it up, using red smoke as an ink. It said:

LESTER WHITE BULL
NEEDS YOUR HELF

"Cute," said Todd, tight-lipped. "One of our own drones, no doubt. Put Sanjay and Chantel Griggs together and there's no telling what they'll come up with. Now look, Beatrice. This is important to me. And if it's important to me, it's important to *you*—and your family. So don't screw it up. We just need to let him see you, so he knows we're for real. Then we'll talk about the exchange. Do as you're told, and everybody goes home happy. Understand?"

"I understand," Beatrice answered. She unbuckled her seat belt. "I'm just not sure I believe you."

"Careful," said her captor, sliding his sunglasses back down over his eyes. "You're going to hurt my feelings."

Lucas Todd stayed in the SUV with his driver, hidden by the vehicle's tinted windows. He opened up a laptop and put on a pair of headphones. Another, smaller laptop sat on the console. In the back of the SUV Beatrice saw a welter of USB cables, three Kevlar vests, and a spare keyboard. Two assault rifles stood in a rack just behind the right rear wheel well.

Beatrice was accompanied by Todd's security men. One of the goons, the music lover, was blonde and blue-eyed. The other was an African American man with close-cropped hair and tiny round ears the size of potato chips. Despite their differing appearances, the men were equally intimidating—hulking, neckless beasts who stood sullen and silent behind their aviator sunglasses. None of the group had a red wristband—the equivalent of a ticket, evidently—but the guards showed IDs to the security personnel who stood at the entrance to the festival gates and, after some discussion, the little group was waived in.

ACL Fest sprawled over two hundred acres of rolling green lawn and live oak trees on a spit of land where Barton Creek flows into the Colorado River—or, as the locals called the river, Lady Bird Lake, after former first lady Lady Bird Johnson. It was an expansive blue day in early October, sunny and mild and as soft as a box of puppies. Even at this hour, early in the afternoon, twenty thousand people filled Zilker Park so completely that it bulged like a Rastafarian's hair net. All around Beatrice and her two guards were men in sandals and shorts, women in gauzy long skirts and cowboy boots, people running, children spinning, the din of shouts in Spanish and German and a score of other languages. The sounds of laughter and amplified music drifted in the air from half a dozen stages standing at various spots across a giant meadow.

Sick with worry—for herself and her family, for Lester White Bull and the kids she'd only met once— Beatrice couldn't help wondering: *Is Lady Gaga here?*

Beatrice and her minders—Thor and Black Panther, she'd named them in her head—made their way slowly through the sea of humanity toward a relatively deserted grove of oaks at the southeastern corner of the park. Once they'd arrived, the security men flanked her as they scanned the crowd for any sign of the kids they were hoping to find. Ten minutes passed. Fifteen. The minders listened to radio messages through the earpieces each wore and finally they conferred with each other.

"*The Russian girl,*" Beatrice heard Black Panther say. The African-American man spoke into the microphone attached to his shirt cuff. "*No sign here…he said twenty minutes…that's a negative.*" She was relieved and disappointed at the same time. Her knees were starting to hurt, so she rocked back and forth on the balls of her feet. She tried to pick out the tune of one of the several songs she could hear reverberating through the park, but the bass notes coming from different directions seemed to cancel each other out. She yawned. *So what if the kids didn't show? What would the next move be? Was Lucas Todd going to let her go home? How long could he possibly hold her without her mother finding out where she was? Surely there were laws about this sort of thing. Eyewitness news investigations. Congressional inquiries. How could this possibly be right?*

Beatrice whirled when she heard the sound of pops off to one side. Her first thought was firecrackers. Then she remembered the first thing *anyone* thought when they heard gunshots was that the gunshots sounded like firecrackers, and she figured maybe it *was* gunshots. The men beside her evidently thought the same thing. They crouched and reached inside their jackets for their weapons. Nothing else happened, though, and the crowd began to move again. When the men straightened up, they saw Mila and Sanjay standing thirty yards in front of them. The Russian girl and the Indian boy grinned and waved, as if daring the two guards to do something about it.

"Hey!" said Black Panther, starting forward. Mila and Sanjay whirled and ran, and the African-American man took off after them.

Thor stood his ground, his head swiveling back and forth to scout the terrain. He spoke excitedly into his shirt cuff, then held his hand to his ear to hear the instructions being radioed back to him. But only for a moment. In the next instant Thor cried out in pain. He swatted the earpiece out of his ear.

Beatrice couldn't explain it.

She heard someone call her name. One second she was looking at an empty space in the shade behind her. The next, Lester White Bull appeared out of nowhere and moved toward her, carrying a blanket, slightly hunched over but walking quickly. He grabbed Beatrice's arm and broke into a run. Beatrice didn't need any instruction. She suspected she was faster than Lester, and her legs ached for exertion.

Still doubled over, Thor lunged at them, but missed.

"Help!" Lester shouted. "HELP US! He's got a gun!"

Beatrice ran faster than she'd ever run in her life. She knew Lucas Todd's goon was after her—after *them*—and she knew she only had one chance. She was nimble and quick and so, surprisingly, was Lester. They threaded through the crowd like wind through a cornfield. Their pursuer wasn't so gentle.

"MOVE!" he was shouting, knocking festival-goers aside.

"Help us!" Lester repeated. "He's trying to kill us!"

And then he said something odd. Screamed it, actually.

"Chantel! Do it NOW!"

Twenty yards ahead of them, standing beside the southernmost cluster of artisan stalls that sold t-shirts, anklets, and patchouli oil, Chantel Griggs clicked her lighter and touched it to the fuses of several sticks of what looked like dynamite.

But these weapons didn't detonate. When the short fuses burned down, the sticks spat out thick plumes of smoke, and Chantel tossed them into the grass directly in front of the fugitives. Billowing clouds of red and green hissed out of each of the canisters, almost instantly hiding Chantel. Lester and Beatrice ducked into the cloud, just a few steps ahead of their pursuer. They burst out again several yards away. At first they thought the distraction had worked. Lester pulled Beatrice close and gave her a hug. That's when Thor reappeared as well. "Run!" they shouted to each other. It wasn't so easy to stay in front this time. Beatrice was starting to tire. She saw young people turn toward them, wide-eyed, taking in the sight of the two kids appearing out of the wall of smoke, fleeing an angry man in a black suit.

Lester headed directly into the Old 97s' audience, knocking people down, leaping over sitting figures, crawling on his hands and knees, still clutching his ridiculous blanket. Beatrice tripped over a backpack and landed in the middle of someone's picnic. She felt Thor's huge hands on her ankles as he dragged her back toward him. She'd lost the race, she realized. She was back in custody. But then something strange happened. The thug was surrounded.

"Let 'em go!" a bystander hollered. He was bare-chested, and wearing a green sombrero.

"Dude!" shouted the woman beside him, trying to place a hula hoop over Thor's head. "Leave her alone!"

The big blond man shoved the woman so hard that she tripped on a stray festival-goer and fell over backward. Enraged, her boyfriend lowered his head and slammed into her attacker. Thor threw the boyfriend off, but the boyfriend had buddies, three of them, who now joined the fight. One of them yanked the pistol from the big blonde man's holster. Another wrapped his arms around Thor's knees and bulled him to the ground. Gasping for breath, Beatrice crawled on all fours through a forest of feet and legs until Lester found her and helped her up. They started to run again, but were brought up short by the figure standing in front of them. He had a head of thick white hair and three days' worth of beard, also white. He wore cargo shorts and a t-shirt that said SCIENCE IS MAGIC FOR SMART PEOPLE. He stretched out his hand. Beatrice could hear the sounds of chaos behind her. Shouting. A chorus of screams.

"Thank God," Lester panted. "I was starting to worry."

"Don't let me stop you. I take it you want to get out of here?"

"Hold on." Lester turned to Beatrice. "Lift up your shirt."

"Excuse me?"

"Please. I need to see your back. It's important."

Beatrice turned, bunched her t-shirt, and lifted with both hands. She felt something like a bandage being peeled from the skin of her upper spine, just above her bra strap.

Lester held up a translucent sticker, about the size of a quarter, with what looked like tiny metallic veins in it.

"Tracking device," he announced. Just then an Austin Parks Department three-wheeler approached, manned by a park ranger and evidently heading for the scene of the commotion. It slowed as it approached the crowd, and Lester reached over and slapped the surveillance device on one fender.

"Clever," said the man who stood facing them. "Now can we go?"

"Beatrice, meet Paul Geiger. And yes. Let's go."

"Hi, Paul Geiger," said Beatrice. Then, to Lester: "You can call me Bea."

Ten: Geiger

"You have documents?" said the man, his voice creeping up an octave as he spoke. "Some kind of proof? I hope you have documents, Lester, because this is one wild-ass story, and my whereabouts are no longer a secret. As you can imagine, I've spent a hell of a lot of time and effort trying to keep them to myself."

They sat in the basement of Paul Geiger's cinder block-walled house somewhere in the cedar-covered hills west of Austin. Beatrice was parked on an age-smeared chintz loveseat, sipping from a cup of Orange Zinger tea and occasionally dipping triangles of pita bread into a bowl of homemade hummus. The kids from the Academy lounged on various pieces of mismatched furniture around her. Victor Cho—sleepy-eyed and silent, as usual—cradled his closed laptop. He looked as if he might be about to sing it a lullabye. Mila was fidgeting with a pack of cigarettes, clearly chafing at their host's pronouncement that no smoking was allowed inside and that she, Mila, was not allowed *outside*. Too dangerous, Geiger said. The Academy was looking for them—and the Academy, aided by elements of the federal government, doubtless had numerous technologies employed in the search. There would be no texts *out*, no emails *in*, no communicating with the outside world in any fashion. In fact, it was best not even to think about the outside world. Beatrice thought the man was kidding about this last piece of advice, but she couldn't be sure.

"Dude," said Sanjay. "You are so old school. We've got something *better* than documents." The lanky Indian boy pulled a flash drive out of the pocket of his robe and reached for Victor's laptop. Victor eyes went wide. It was clear he wasn't accustomed to sharing. But after a moment of hesitation, and a brief duel of nerdy scowls, he handed Sanjay the machine. Sanjay inserted the little stick in the USB port. He clicked on a thumbnail image and a video popped up on the screen. It was Lucas Todd, wearing his trademark sweater vest.

"Watch this."

The kids crowded around a ripped leather sofa to look over Sanjay's shoulder. At first there was nothing menacing in the video. Lucas Todd was old, of course—at least forty-five—and old is not attractive. Old means death, decay, and the gradual inability to dance. And yet even Beatrice had to admit to herself that he seemed like a trustworthy sort, apparently sincere, obviously intelligent. His diction was impeccable. In fact, if you weren't paying attention, it was easy to glide over what he was saying because he sounded so good saying it. Surely it was reasonable—whatever it was. Surely it made sense. Surely it was going to benefit everyone.

Everyone who *survived*, that is.

"See?" said Lester, when the clip ended. "Sanjay's right. This is better. Victor managed to break through one of their firewalls and grab like, a truckload of their documents and videos."

"Good Lord." Paul Geiger grabbed the skin of his own cheeks and pulled them down so the insides of his eyelids showed. "Lucas Todd has checked out of reality as we know it."

"He's a nut job," Chantel confirmed. "I told y'all that."

A doomed silence fell over the room.

For a moment, at least.

"I'm sorry," said Beatrice. "Do you guys really have any idea what he's talking about? Because I don't."

"Yes," said Geiger. He was a short, slightly built man, in his early fifties maybe, with bushy eyebrows and a wide mouth. He spoke and gestured rapidly, and was given to running a hand back through his mane of white hair as he pondered some new difficulty or dilemma. He was barefoot, and he'd exchanged his SCIENCE IS MAGIC t-shirt for a blue linen button-down, but he still wore faded green cargo shorts and a welter of bracelets on his left wrist. He'd been chomping on a celery stick when he entered the room, only now it had become a pointer, which he used to punctuate his sentences. He began to pace back and forth on the carpet in front of them like a wolf in a cage, periodically pausing to gaze or glare at his guests as if they were a gaggle of unruly undergraduates.

"I think I *do* know what he's talking about, as a matter of fact. The end of the world." Geiger went to one of the two windows that faced east. He stuck two fingers between the slats of the blinds and gazed out over the hills toward the Capitol, the University of Texas tower, and the giant bank and condominium buildings downtown. "Lucas Todd and his friends—and he has some very influential friends, I might add—think of themselves as saviors. I suspected that already, but the clip we just saw makes it clear. And like all saviors, they think the rest of us need them to make our decisions for us. This is a fantastic planet, kids. It's a fantastic *event*, really: a crazy intersection of physics and organic chemistry and sheer dumb luck that somehow produced a ball of water and light and warmth in the midst of the barbarous vast emptiness of cold and darkness we call *space*. We, humanity, are inheritors of the biggest golden ticket that's ever been issued. And what have we done? Huh? Seriously. What have we done, my friends, with our beautiful, mysterious, incredible earth?"

"Um," said Chantel. "Screwed it up?"

"SCREWED IT UP! Oh yes! Screwed it up royally! We've turned our little blue dot in the great grim sea of nothingness into a pig sty. There are seven and a half billion people on the planet today, with estimates we'll hit *nine* billion in the next twenty years. In the United States alone we generate 260 million tons of garbage a year, and some of my fellow scientists estimate we throw away enough plastic every year to circle the earth *four times over*. Plastic. A substance that doesn't disintegrate. Doesn't biodegrade. Doesn't *go* anywhere. We are destroying the rain forests at a rate of thirty thousand square miles per year, and in the past fifteen years we've reduced the number of animals living in the wild by half. The planet is warmer than at any time in recorded history, more crowded than it's ever been, dirtier than ever, more toxic, more rutted, more frantic. There are people out there—the Finnish philosopher and fisherman Pennti Linkola, for example—who think enough is enough. That we're destroying the planet. Not in theory. Not at some point in the future. *Now*. I know for a fact that Lucas Todd has read and corresponded with Linkola. He's read the anti-technology philosopher and serial bomber Ted Kaczynski. He's always had a fascination with these fanatics. In the past, though, it was academic. Now it's real, and he's no longer content to wait. What Lucas Todd and his followers want to do is restore the balance."

"Right," said Mila. "By taking us out of equation."

"Depopulation, writ large."

"What do you mean," asked Beatrice, "by *depopulation*?"

"Yes," said Mila. "Stop speaking English. It confuses her."

"There's no need for that, Mila. Beatrice, the words come from Latin. *De*, meaning to take away from. Population, from the root word *populus*, or people."

"De-*people*?"

"Exactly. Get rid of the people."

"By exterminating us," said Lester. "There's no sense in sugar-coating it. You can call it whatever you want, but the bottom line is this: Lucas Todd and his friends want to lighten the load. They want solitude. They want wide open spaces. Clean air. Fresh water. A dark sky at night. They propose to save the planet by killing *billions* of people."

"Okay," said Beatrice. "I get it. But even assuming all of this is true, how are they going to do it?"

Geiger snorted. He seemed grimly amused, as if the answer were some inside secret gone sideways. "Good question! Yes! GREAT question. It's not a matter of magical rhinestones, like in the movies. It ain't going to happen with the snap of anyone's fingers. It's pathogens, my dear. *Germs.* The American military has acquired and maintains active and aggressive cultures of some of the world's most effective killers. Anthrax. Ebola. Cholera. Smallpox. In a way, these are the ideal weapons for our friends at the Academy. Their effects on the human body mimic the effect of humanity on Earth. The pathogens aren't intending to damage their host, after all. They aren't intending anything except their own propagation. But they kill nevertheless. The Ebola virus was first identified in West Africa in the 1970s. Once the virus settles in, it slowly converts the body's collagen to mush, liquefying the under-layers of skin. Clots thicken the bloodstream and cause internal and external hemorrhaging—frequently from the eyes. Death results after the body is basically drained of blood from the *inside.* And death does come: the mortality rate for the various strains of Ebola are estimated to be somewhere between fifty and ninety percent. Anthrax is another very effective murderer. It generally kills only when inhaled. The spores are picked up by microphages in the lungs and transported to the lymph nodes. Maturing along the way, they turn into bacteria, and generate lethal doses of chemicals that ordinarily wouldn't be harmful at all. Death comes in days. Sometimes sooner. And the Plague? Have you studied that one, Beatrice? It killed half the population of Europe seven hundred years ago. The bacteria, *Yersinia pestis,* go undercover in the human body until they can get to safety in the lymph nodes, where they replicate themselves so effectively that the immune system basically destroys its own body, driving the victim into septic shock—but not until he or she has sprouted black bulbs of blood and pus the size and consistency of hard-boiled eggs. These are the weapons our friends at the Academy plan to use. And they know how and when to disburse them to achieve maximum depopulation."

"When, though? Like, soon?"

Lester nodded. "Like, very soon. Victor's hacked into the Academy's encrypted communications. The germ caches are already deployed, apparently."

"And all this happens through spreading a disease." Beatrice meant to have asked a question, but the implications of what she was hearing were starting to set in. Her voice was strained and flat.

"*Diseases*, plural. You name it. Start with the three we just mentioned, and let your imagination fill in the rest. Smallpox. Dengue. The Marburg virus. COVID-19. Then leave a couple of blanks for whatever nasty bugs the Russians have managed to capture melting out of the permafrost in Siberia."

Beatrice searched for comfort in the faces around her. None was offered. "That doesn't make any sense. We already *have* all those diseases. They're under control, right? They're not killing everybody."

"In various places, yes, they're under control. But we're talking about concentrated disbursements of pathogens in highly populous areas. Areas that haven't been exposed to these illnesses in the recent past. Lucas and his associates know how to do it. They've got genetic and geographic profiles of every significant ethnic group in the world. Trust me. I helped them figure it out."

Even Victor Cho looked up.

"You did what?" said Chantel.

"I helped them."

Now Mila, speaking with the voice of one betrayed: "Why, Paul Geiger?"

The little man ran his hands back through his hair. He seemed to wince at the ugliness of his own memories. "In fact, I didn't just help them. I *taught* them."

Beatrice shook her head.

"But it wasn't real back then," said Geiger. "It was modeling. It was studying the theoretical effects of pathogen releases in different regions, under various climatic and seasonal circumstances, and released into different genetic populations. We looked it. The Russians did it, and we assume the Chinese did, too, though we couldn't prove it. But again, it was all modeling. War games stuff. Trying to prepare for a worst-case scenario in case another country tried to use biological weapons against *us*. But these guys… Jesus. Obviously it's not a game anymore. Lucas Todd and his co-conspirators somehow lost sight of the fact that there are actual human lives in back of all these numbers. That science has real consequences. Very real, and potentially very bloody, consequences."

"Isn't there anything we can do?" said Beatrice. "What about the police?"

"We have to go to somebody," Geiger agreed, pausing to sample a carrot end's worth of hummus. "We can't fix this ourselves. The problem is, who? How do we make sure we're delivering this information to the right people? I mean, Lucas Todd is smart, but he's only one man. He answers to someone else. I've always suspected it. And he has to have a lot of help to do what he wants to do. The military. The CDC. The CIA. Who knows how deep this goes? And not just here. Not just in the *U.S.* I suspect he has allies in other governments as well."

"We know he does," said Chantel. "We've got emails back and forth between the Academy and people in China, in Russia, Brazil, Vietnam, you name it."

"So maybe we send *our* information to multiple people as well," said Lester.

"Multiple people."

"Like, *tons* of people. A mass data dump. We know some of the wrong people will get it. But we're bound to get it to some of the right ones as well."

"Hey," said Sanjay. His eyes lit up with excitement. "That gives me an idea."

Eleven: The Trap

"Larry," said Anne McIlvaine, "I don't *care* if you disagree with me. I can't wait any longer. I've got to tell someone about Bea. It's been two days. Two days without a word. That's not like her, and you know it. And it can't be legal."

"Two days? Already?"

"Yes. Trust me. I can count to two. And I don't want any of that damn tea."

"Yeah," said Frankie, standing in one corner of the kitchen. "Cut it out with the tea. It's nasty. And it makes me sleepy."

"Mind your manners, son. We need to stay calm for your mother."

Anne shook her head. "Calm is no longer an option. Calm is for when your cat disappears, not your daughter. I've called Channel 13. The reporter said she's on her way. Do you have a better idea? The FBI doesn't seem to have any answers."

"I'm sorry to hear that."

"Sorry to hear what?"

"You said a reporter was coming. I can't allow you to talk to the media. I'm sorry, Anne."

"Sorry? What do you mean, you're sorry? Since when is it up to you?"

"Since now."

Larry pushed back his chair and took up a position at the doorway between the kitchen and the living room.

Anne's eyes blazed. "Oh my God. Wait a minute. You're...you're with *them*, aren't you?"

Larry spoke with a tone of exaggerated patience. "How do you mean? With whom?"

"You're working for the people who took Bea. I had a weird feeling about that when you said Beatrice is special. That's what *they* said, when they came to talk to her after she had her whole basilisk thing."

Larry raised his eyebrows. "And nothing bad happened then, did it?'"

"No. And nothing bad's going to happen now either, because I'm getting my daughter back."

"She's safe. That's all you need to know. She's safe, and—"

Anne's chair scraped the floor as she stood. "No, that's *not* all I need to know. Where is she? She's got to be going crazy worrying about us."

"She's had the same thing you've had."

"A sedative? Oh my God. That's a huge mistake. You know she's not normal. Her mind—it's not... I don't know how to say this, but they tried putting her on sedatives after the dragon episode. Xanax. Klonopin. It just makes things worse. It's like putting a blanket on a bear. You're just going to wake up something very powerful that you don't want awake. For God's sake, Larry—"

Anne stopped short when the doorbell rang.

Larry wagged his head. "Damn it, Anne. What have you done?"

"I told you what I've done. Now move."

"Stay here," said Larry. He drew a small semi-automatic pistol out of a holster hidden beneath his hoodie. "You too, Frank. One word out of either of you, and Beatrice is going to find herself in a world of hurt. I'll take care of this."

Anne shook her head in disgust. "Jesus. You've been a liar and a spy this whole time. And I've been letting you get away with it."

"I'm not a spy. I'm a soldier, in a much bigger war than you can possibly imagine. Please. For everyone's sake. Keep your mouth shut."

Larry padded to the front door. He turned to make sure Anne and Frankie were a safe distance away, then hid the pistol behind his back and yanked the door open. He knew how to handle reporters. *Indignation. Firmness. Get off my lawn.* But he wasn't quite prepared for what he saw next. Nine firemen—and one firewoman—stood on Anne's porch. They'd been to the house before, and they considered Anne McIlvaine to be part of their extended family.

Their leader was a burly former Howard Payne University defensive tackle named Harold "Boots" Blattner. He stood six feet four and tipped the scales at 230 pounds. His hands were the size of horseshoe crabs.

"Who are you?" said Larry Bartkowski. "What do you want?"

"We fight fires," said the big man. "City of Houston, Stations 93, 18, and 24. Union of Firefighters Local No. 151. Used to work with Anne's husband. I'm Boots Blattner, and I need to see Anne."

"Afraid not," said Bartkowski dismissively. "I'm a federal agent. This is a national security matter."

"Yeah? Since when is kidnapping a teenage girl a national security matter? Don't act surprised. Anne told us all about it. This man here used to work for the FBI, didn't you Bobby? He still has buddies in the Bureau, and they say they've never *heard* of a federal agent named Gary Bratkowski."

"Larry Bartkowski."

"That's what I said. *Gary Bratkowski.* So we're coming in, whether you like it or not. And if it turns out you've hurt a single hair on that little girl's head, you're gonna regret it for the rest of your natural life, you lying sack of garbage. Anne!?! Are you in there?"

Bartkowski leveled the pistol at Blattner's forehead. "I told you, you're not—"

But he never had a chance to finish the sentence. Anne McIlvaine brought an earthenware vase down on Larry Bartkowski's head. The vase shattered. Larry's skull held firm, but he staggered under the blow. Before he could recover his senses, Boots Blattner had wrestled the pistol away from the man and slammed him to the floor.

"Here's the number," said Blattner, handing Beatrice's mother a yellow Post-It with several digits scrawled in red ink. He held one of Larry's wrists with the other hand. He had a heel on Larry's neck. "That's the real FBI. I suggest you call 'em, ASAP. We'll take care of John Wick here."

Now it was Larry Bartkowski's turn to be outraged. Disarmed and kissing a section of cracked linoleum, he looked up at the faces of Houston's finest. The finest weren't happy. And the finest, it turned out, were wearing steel-toed footwear.

Twelve: Lester's Confession

Beatrice sat two feet from Lester on Paul Geiger's grungy leather sofa. The other kids had vacated the room. Forbidden from using his laptop, Victor Cho lurked in the kitchen, sipping an energy drink that looked like anti-freeze and monitoring traffic on Paul's police scanner. Mila was downstairs in the basement with a window open, sucking on a cancer stick. Chantel was busy in the garage, constructing a mechanical thingamabob with a number of electronic components, though she'd declined to discuss the nature of the project. Sanjay and Paul Geiger were off in another corner of the rambling house, plotting against Lucas Todd.

It was an unseasonably warm night, and, since their host didn't believe in air conditioning, Lester had opened two of the windows to catch a breeze. Outside they could hear the buzz of cicadas, the tinkle of chimes and, periodically, the rotors of a helicopter passing over the neighborhood.

"How did you know he would be there?" asked Beatrice.

Lester set down the book he'd been pretending to read. "At ACL? It was just a guess. But Paul's a music freak, especially live music, and he hasn't missed a Luddite show in years. He's old friends with Ban MacAvoy, the lead singer, from when they went to college together in England. He's also a big fan of Larry Gilbert and the Department of Integrative Biology at UT, and I knew he'd done his graduate studies in Austin, so it just made sense."

"Thank God he found us when he did. He likes you, you know. I can tell."

"He's the closest thing I've ever had to a dad. And even he wasn't that close. But it was something."

"Why did you leave the Academy, by the way? I was there, you know. They took me there. It's beautiful."

"Sure, it's beautiful, if you're doing what they want you do to. If you're on board for their whole Smart-People-Rule-the-World agenda. But I got sick of it. They had me destroying records online. When I said I wasn't going to do it anymore, they started trying to figure out how they were going to get rid of me. They threatened to ship me and Mila off to their auxiliary academy. Some dump in Oklahoma. We weren't sure how long we were going to be there, and no one would tell us. We didn't like our chances, so we took off."

"You took off with some of their stuff, is what I heard. Is that why Lucas Todd is so mad?"

"Some of their *stuff.* Yes. Like, high tech weaponry. Experimental, mostly, though some of it is pretty close to being battlefield ready. But it'll be a while before they figure out exactly what we took. Victor and I went in and did some record destruction of our own. They trained me well."

"What kind of records did they have you deleting?"

"Bank records. Birth certificates. Real estate deeds. You name it. It was supposed to be, like, a game. A test. To see if I could do it. And of course I could. It was easy. But no one would ever tell me why."

"But you figured it out."

"I figured out a couple of things. One was that what we were supposed to be pretending to do was disruption of an enemy society."

"And the other?" Beatrice asked.

"That was a little weirder. They had me destroying our *own* records. Mila. Victor. Me. We no longer exist, at least officially. And if you don't exist, who knows if you're gone?"

"Well, that brings up another question."

"Shoot," said Lester.

"How did you do that thing today?"

"What thing?"

"You know what thing. The thing where you just *appeared* out of thin air."

Lester nodded. The hint of a smile played on his lips. "Ah, yes. My invisibility cloak."

"You're joking. Right?"

"I'm not joking. It's one of the items Lucas Todd is desperate to get back. We borrowed it from him. But he borrowed it from DARPA, and I'm pretty sure they're going to like, ask him about it one of these days."

"But…an *invisibility cloak*? I thought you guys were all about science. And what's DARPA?"

"DARPA is the government's Defense Advanced Research Projects Agency. The mad scientists. And my little blanket *is* science. It's all just a matter of bending light. It's actually fairly easy in a lab—a little tougher out in the field. The cloak is constructed so three-dimensional objects appear flat. At the same time, the fibers on one side of the cloak are streaming video signals to the other side in real time, so that what would be visible on the back is streamed to the front. So it's like you're looking straight through it."

"Invisible."

"Exactly. Eventually, we'll all have one. Kids will wrap themselves up in them at night so the monsters can't get them. Teenagers will use 'em for, like… Never mind."

"And the smoke bombs?"

"That was Chantel's deal. Nothing fancy. Potassium nitrate and sugar, mostly, packed into cardboard paper towel cylinders. You just heat the ingredients, mix 'em up, pack the stuff in the cylinders and wait for your opportunity. Same basic stuff she used for the drone writing. Chantel is hella smart, Beatrice. Don't get her mad at you. She'll build a bunch of robot spiders and program them to hunt you for the rest of your life. Even Mila isn't crazy enough to mess with Chantel."

Beatrice bit her lip. She wasn't sure how to say what she wanted to say next. She pulled her elbows in close to her body, as if they were armor.

"So…why? I mean, why me?"

Lester reached for the book again. It was a collection of black and white photographs of ancient country and western singers: Johnny Cash, Willie Nelson, and a bunch of others she didn't recognize. Stone Age stuff.

"Why you?" he said. But clearly he knew what she meant. She could see blotches of pink on the skin at the base of his throat. "God. They showed you my room, didn't they?"

She nodded. "I wasn't sure whether I should be flattered or, *you know*. Just call the cops."

He winced, still avoiding her eyes. "Me neither. I don't know why. You spend all your time with technology. You think you know how everything works. How everything is supposed to work, right? And then one day you realize you've been thinking about someone so much you forgot to eat. Like, you forget what you're supposed to be doing. And none of it makes sense and all of it makes sense and…I don't even know you. Trust me. I didn't *plan* it." Lester looked down at his hands. "Do you have a boyfriend?"

Beatrice fought off a rueful smile.

"No boyfriend. It's the hair, I think."

Lester gazed at her, puzzled. "You have beautiful hair. Like a torch, or something."

Now it was Beatrice's turn to blush. "And the ear piece? When the security guy got distracted?"

"You mean in the park? That was Victor. He and Sanjay hacked into the Academy's radio signal and poured a whole lot of distortion into that frequency all at once. Enough to bust an eardrum, anyway. Then it was just a matter of running. You and I found Paul. Or he found us. Once I slapped that tracker decal on the three-wheeler, the Academy's goons starting following it instead of you. You saw how crowded it was in there. It's impossible to keep tabs on anyone visually. The rest of the group just walked out of the park and like, hung around at Barton Springs until Paul went and picked them up."

A torch, thought Beatrice. *My hair is a torch.*

She wasn't exactly sure what it meant, but it sounded like the nicest thing a boy had ever said to her. "Like a torch," she murmured. She hadn't actually meant to say it. She thought she was just thinking it. But her mind was a strange mechanism, and sometimes it made things happen that she didn't mean to have happen.

Lester gazed at her for a good long while before he leaned toward her. His eyes held a weird kind of light. Then his hand was on hers, warm and heavy and somehow the center of the room.

"You were the only bright thing in my life for a long time," he said, so softly that she could barely hear him. "I know you're trying to pretend you're nothing out of the ordinary. But I also know it isn't true. You have a family. A real family. And that's the normal part of your life, but it's not all of it. You can like, call up *dragons*. And then…you know. Destroy them. You're a super hero, Beatrice. Bea. And one of these days, everyone's gonna realize it."

"I didn't mean to…with the dragon. You know that, right? I didn't want it."

"No. I get it. Who would want it? But it happened. I know it did. And that makes you a wizard. Only for real." He raised his eyebrows. Grinned. "So how about it? How about we go to Hogwarts sometime?"

She couldn't help laughing. "Don't let Mila hear you say that! That's blasphemy."

"Hey. I'm a scientist too. A wannabe scientist, anyway. But a little magic never hurt anyone."

"No," she agreed. "Probably not."

He kissed her then, and she wondered what she would do but really she didn't do much because she was so amazed and confused by the sensation. She felt something between delight and panic, or maybe something on the far side of both, and her heart was pounding and she closed her eyes and her eyelids seemed to be glowing. But then there was a noise in the hallway just outside the door and Lester pulled back. Beatrice looked down, and the moment passed.

"So who is this guy?" said Beatrice, when she'd regained her composure. She gestured around the room at the electric guitars mounted on the walls, the posters of The Clash and The Jam and various other musical common nouns.

"I don't know. He's just Paul Geiger to me. Biologist. Genius. Singer-songwriter. Don't let him get you alone with one of those guitars. It's painful. He's got a song he likes to sing about *Escherichia coli*. But yes. Genius. When I got to the Academy, we all worked with Paul. He disappeared like, three years ago. Which really sucked, because he was the only person there who ever seemed to think about anyone other than himself."

"Is he okay? Can you trust him?"

"You tell me."

"What's that supposed to mean?"

"It means you have something we don't have. You have emotional assets we lack. So, seriously. You tell me. Does this feel right?

Beatrice shrugged. "Except for the fact that you were out there creeping on my Instagram for several months, I guess it feels right. Paul feels right, anyway. He seems honest. Where did he go? I mean, when he left the school."

"Well, *here*, I guess. But no one knew for sure. In fact, no one at the Academy would even let on that he'd gone."

"This is Academy way," announced Mila, entering the room. "Also Stalinist way. Paul Geiger disappears from all photographs, like smoke mirage. Anything he ever signed or wrote or was part of is erased. Like we all will be, if we are not being careful. Why you are sitting in so much near closeness, by the way? Couch is larger than Moscow bus. There is plenty of room."

Lester shot Beatrice a rueful look as he scooted back across the scuffed leather. "People come and go at the

Academy. There's no rhyme or reason to it. And no one bothers to tell you why."

"What did he do there?"

"Like I said. He was a biologist. Made his name back in the Nineties studying airborne pathogens."

"Pathogens," Mila explained. "*Germs.*"

Beatrice shook her head. "I get it. Thank you. So he was the boss?"

"No. You've met the boss. Lucas Todd. Real asshole. A by-the-books kind of guy. Smiles and sweater vests. Handshakes and head games. He always acted like he knew who you were. 'Cause he was the one who really cared about you, right? But his eyes were empty. And trust me, his heart is empty too."

"And you really think this depopulation thing is what they're trying to do?"

"I don't just think it. I know it. Like Paul said, there are over seven billion people in the world today. The target is to eliminate four fifths of them. It's right there in their texts and emails. The English was easy. Victor's got enough Mandarin to figure out what they're talking about with the People's Republic, and Mila has translated the stuff that was in Russian and Arabic."

Beatrice squinted. Her gaze went to the floor as she tried to work out the numbers.

"You're American," said Mila "So l am helping you with math. Four fifths of seven billion. That's like, a *lot.*"

"So we tell the police."

"Right."

"We like, tell the *President.*"

"How?"

"Letter?" said Beatrice. "Email?"

"Both methods," said Mila, "are over-watched by government computer-type eyeballs. Government is not our friend."

"Parts of it might be," Lester corrected her. "We don't know. But parts of it are definitely not—like the part that flies those damned helicopters, for example. And the problem is, it's getting late. According to Victor, Lucas Todd and his friends have already deployed their caches of pathogens in various parts of the world. Sub-Saharan Africa. Western China. Parts of India. Most of these pathogens are only toxic to humans, so there's no collateral damage. No toxic clouds. No radioactive seas. Just mountains of dead bodies. They make things nasty for a few years, then they go away. Not completely, or course—but enough. And the world that remains is considerably lighter."

"Lighter?"

"That's what they call it."

"Like it's carrying us," said Mila.

"Well, and of course it is, if you think about it. But with disease, the earth regenerates. And huge chunks of territory are left wide open, waiting to be claimed by whoever is well organized and well-armed enough to take them. It helps that official records are going to be wiped out all across the world at more or less the same time." Lester shook his head. "Thanks, in part, to me."

"So they're doing this to save the environment?"

"Not at all. They're doing this because they're sick bastards. You don't save the environment by murdering human beings. We're PART of the environment. We live here too. How do you claim to love the earth—to love *life*—and still plan to murder your fellow man?"

"And woman," said Mila.

"No, I'm with you. I get it. But how do we stop them?"

"That's what Paul's working on. I hope."

"And why kids? I mean, why did the Academy have teenagers working on stuff like this in the first place?"

"Because young people—kids—have the kind of brains they want. The teenage brain is an amazing thing. It's expanding and absorbing information at an incredible rate. There are no limits. A lot of the most original thinking of the past several centuries has come from kids who didn't know they weren't supposed to be able to do what they were doing. They just did it. Look at Mozart, right? Writing symphonies at the age of eight. Look at Louis Braille inventing his brilliant language for the blind when he was fifteen, and at Joseph Bombardier and Samuel Colt and Blaise Pascal. Look at Kelvin Doe and Ashton Cofer, Philo Farnsworth—the kid who invented TV—and Boyan Slat. Look at Shuster and Siegel, for that matter. The inventors of Superman! The potential's always been there. It's just never been harnessed. Or whatever the right word is."

"*Captured*," said Mila.

"What about *nurtured*?" said Beatrice.

"Nope. Probably *captured*."

"And remember, Academy kids don't have a whole lot going on in their lives. There's no one to miss us. No distractions. No one to worry about."

Beatrice winced. "Never?"

"We're society's garbage, Bea. Nobody cares. Sometimes there's a long-lost uncle out there who does some poking around, or a cousin who starts asking questions. Not in my case, of course. But sometimes. And the fact is, they can be managed."

"Managed how?"

"Money. Lies. Government bullshit. Your mother was probably told you were contacted by a terrorist cell—coed jihadis in a plumbing van; it happens all the time, right?—and the government took you into custody to ask you a few questions. For your own safety, of course. That's all she knows."

"I need to talk to her, Lester."

"You can't."

"Please. Look, my family's not exactly at the top of the food chain either. We live in a duplex next to the water treatment plant. I'm still using an iPhone 6. I need to warn her. Can you help me?"

"Trust me. It's better for her that you not contact her."

"We have a plan!" said Paul Geiger from the next room. A moment later, he and Sanjay entered. Victor and Chantel piled in behind them.

"It's going to take every minute of the next twenty-four—scratch that—twenty-*one* hours. And we're going to have to work very hard. But it just might work."

"We're going to a music festival," said Sanjay.

"We just escaped from a music festival," protested Lester.

"Well, then," said Geiger. A sly grin spread across his face. "You know the way."

"I only have one request," said Chantel. "I know this is going to be dangerous. We're all in big trouble. But I want you to promise me one thing."

"You got it," said Lester.

"Of course," said Sanjay.

The others nodded with grim sincerity.

"Whatever else happens out there," said Chantel. "Don't make me listen to dubstep."

"Look. Here's what we know. Lucas Todd and his thugs are looking for us. He didn't have enough men to watch all the exits today, but he's learned his lesson. He's probably got another ten of his thugs here in Austin by now, plus a dozen more manning remote surveillance and communications monitors back at the Academy. But he's in a difficult spot. I take it from Lester and Victor that he doesn't know we have him on video, talking about Doomsday. Everyone agree?"

There were nods around the room.

"All he knows is that you ran away and took some of his toys—hardware he's accountable for to the boys back at the Pentagon. The cloak, for example. Can I see that, by the way?"

"No," said Mila, grim-faced and pale. "You can't see it. Is invisibility cloak."

"Really? Far out."

"Not really. I am making joke. Please to continue with plan."

"Right. The plan. Todd knows you want out, and he knows you have leverage, especially now that he's lost Beatrice. So he's thinking you all want to make a deal: you give up the toys in exchange for a full release from the Academy. A hall pass for life."

"I'll take it," said Chantel. "Sign me up."

"But there are two complicating factors. One, Lucas Todd will say whatever he needs to say to get his hardware back. But you know, and I know, he'll never *really* let you go. In the back of his mind he suspects you know what he's up to, and that suspicion is going to be enough to get you killed."

"He could do it, too," said Sanjay. "He's got those eyes. All empty and cold and shit."

"He's talking about infecting huge portions of the world's population with a variety of deadly diseases," said Geiger. "You're not even a *gnat* to him. None of us are."

"Okay, so what's the other factor?"

"The other factor is, we don't want to make that trade. We want to bring his ass down. And Lucas Todd doesn't play nice, so we can't either. We've got to make this as big and painful for him as possible."

"Truth," muttered Chantel.

"Right," said Lester, glancing sidelong at Beatrice. He knew she couldn't help it. She was thinking about her mother, and bright tears streaked her face. "I'm up for that."

"Good," said Geiger. "Kids, I'm not gonna candy-coat it. We've got to make this plan work. Because if we don't, a whole lot of people are going to die in very unpleasant ways, and the world is really going to suck."

"Is that your version of a motivational speech?" said Chantel.

"I'm afraid it is. The only good news I have is this: Beatrice, you're free to go."

"Go?" said Bea.

"Sure. This isn't your fight. I'd rather keep you here, for the sake of secrecy, but that's not really my call. I can take you downtown and put you on a bus for Houston, if you'd like. We can buy you a burner phone."

"No," she said.

"No what?" said Lester.

"It's too late. I think my mom would understand. I know my dad would. This *is* my fight. I'm staying."

For some reason they all looked to Mila. She sat at one end of the big couch, biting her nails.

"Somebody is watching too many cowboy movies," she said. Then she glanced at Beatrice and shrugged. "But okay. She stays."

Thirteen: Reunion (Redux)

The next day dawned fair and warm over Austin, but as the morning wore on a north wind filtered into central Texas. The temperature dropped twenty degrees, and the sky went gunmetal gray.

The weather matched Beatrice's mood. She'd had a bad night sleeping on a hard floor, worried about her new friends. The glow of her conversation with Lester had faded. She tossed and turned and dreamt sour dreams. In one of them she woke in an empty city. She wandered through the streets until she heard voices calling out to each other. The calls became cries as she got closer. She turned a corner and looked out on a vast square full of people lying on white sheets. A field of sick people. Of *dying* people. Hundreds of them, and no one in sight to care for them. Some of the faces were black and swollen. Others were lifeless and pale, webbed by lines of blood. Two children were down on their hands and knees, throwing up in front of her. There was a billboard in the distance, with a picture of a beautiful beach and the logo COME TO GALVESTON. One of the children reached out to her, but Beatrice found herself unable to lift her arms. She shuddered with the effort. Her heart thumped inside her like an angry animal, but she couldn't speak. She woke up panicked and despairing, knowing she hadn't helped a single soul. Her palms were wet with sweat.

Victor Cho stood over her. He held a finger to his lips.

"It's okay," he murmured, spreading another blanket over her. "You're safe."

"What happened?"

"I was going to ask *you*," said Victor. "It felt like an earthquake or something. A tremor."

"In Texas?"

He shrugged. "Whatever it was, it's over now."

She spent the morning in hiding, eating bachelor breakfast foods—day-old hummus and prehistoric tortilla chips, a Diet Dr. Pepper and an almost-expired mango yogurt. Hiding didn't come easy to Beatrice. Like her father, she was more inclined to confront a threat than to avoid it, to stand up and take the consequences, whatever they might be. It was easier that way. And quicker. But here the consequences weren't just applicable to her, she realized, so she did her best to sit still. She wasn't the only one who was nervous. Mila looked like she hadn't slept in a week.

The plan was simple. Lester and Paul Geiger had left early in the morning to visit a coffee shop, where they sent a message to Lucas Todd. *Meet at the concert*, it said. *The Luddites. 6 p.m., Toshiba stage.* There Lester would hand over the keys to the plumbing van, which Chantel and Sanjay had hidden in a parking facility downtown. The vehicle still held most of the DARPA gadgets Lucas Todd was anxious to get back. The invisibility cloak and several small drones would be left at a location to be discussed at the meeting. In return, Todd and Geiger would make a little movie together—a brief cellphone video in which Lucas Todd recited that the kids from the Academy were released from their obligations to the federal government without reservation, and free to do as they chose.

No give-backs, no take-backs.

No veiled threats.

And things went just fine. But only for a few minutes.

It wasn't long after Paul and Lester left that morning that the men in the black SUVs arrived. They rolled up silently and parked seventy-five yards down the street. At precisely 10:45 a.m., eight agents of the Academy's security force approached the house with shotguns and M4 carbines at the ready. Another four went around back. The group in front blew the door off its hinges with a hydraulic jack, entered, and wrestled Sanjay and Victor to the kitchen floor. Beatrice, Mila, and Chantel were watching *Red Dawn* on DVD when they heard the blast. Mila picked up a beer bottle to use as a weapon. She dropped it when she saw the guns.

And so it was that a few hours later, the five kids—the four Academy fugitives plus Beatrice, but minus Lester—stood near the front of a festive ACL crowd of several thousand people waiting for the Luddites to appear. They were captives, penned in on either side by Lucas Todd and four of his oversized goons. Thor and Black Panther were two members of the security detail. They were joined by two additional white men, both of whom wore crew cuts, frowns, and very big watches.

Beatrice watched the sky grow dark in the northwest as the cold front moved in. She thought she recognized the rumble of thunder, but it was hard to tell exactly what she was hearing above the sounds of hip-hop and bluegrass, *norteno* and EDM stacked up in the air around them like planes circling a busy airport. Their guards stood glowering and unimpressed beside the kids, weapons tucked into the holsters they wore slung across their shoulders, barely concealed beneath their sports jackets.

"Make a move," said Lucas Todd, locking eyes with each of his hostages in turn. The kinder, gentler Lucas Todd was long gone. This version of the Academy's director had eyes as hard as stone. "Just *one*. And someone gets hurt."

Mila shot him the Italian digit.

Beatrice was just about to say something cutting when Ban MacAvoy strode out onto the stage. Though he was an international star, front man for a two-time Grammy award-winning band and the author of something like three hundred songs, his appearance was so unexpected that only a few people started clapping. He was smaller in person than Beatrice had expected: maybe five foot six, with short red hair and a face that was almost as freckled as hers. He wore black boots and a black leather jacket over a mostly unbuttoned royal blue shirt.

"Austin, Texas!" he shouted, when he'd made it to the mike. A cheer greeted his statement, as folks turned to face the stage. "AUSTIN, TEXAS! Howdy! Did I say that right? My name is BAN MACAVOY." Another pause. The seasoned showman waited for his audience's complete attention. The raucous cheering finally died down. "I know you're here for the music. That's what I'm here for too. But I have something I want to SHOW you. Trust me! You know I'm an advocate for Green Peace. Yes? You know I care as much as you do about the fate of this planet. Am I right? I thought so. So bear with me one minute here."

MacAvoy gazed over to where his sound and light technicians sat on one side of the stage. Beatrice glanced around as well. The crowd seemed puzzled, but not particularly interested. And Lucas Todd, scanning the throng around him for signs of Lester White Bull, was barely paying attention at all.

"Right! I think we're ready. If you have a phone, get it out. Get your camera ready. That's right. Cameras up! Because you're going to want to RECORD this!"

The slender Irishman turned to look at the gigantic screen behind him. He raised his hand as a signal to some unseen techie and a video started to play. The giant screen behind the stage filled with an image of the man beside her: Lucas Todd, looking dapper and collegiate in his clear-framed glasses and an emerald sweater vest. The two smaller screens mounted on the scaffolding on either side of the stage showed the same image. Todd was paying attention now. A moment later, Beatrice realized with a skip of her heart that it was the same footage she'd watched at Paul Geiger's house the previous evening—the footage that revealed Lucas Todd and his associates around the world as well-dressed, cold-blooded murderers. Things were about to get complicated.

In the clip, Lucas Todd stood at a wooden lectern with no label on it. He drank from a bottle of water, and then began. Or, rather, *resumed*, as it appeared he had already been speaking for some time:

> *The Earth has reached its carrying capacity. In fact, it is beyond its carrying capacity. It needs to be cleansed. Lightened. Redeemed. And we who are gathered in this room today, from five continents and twenty-two nations, are the people who can do it. When we give the signal, sometime a little later this year, the deadliest pathogens known to mankind will be released at a hundred and forty locations around the globe—locations picked by us to achieve maximum mortality rates. You know which of the locations are your responsibility. You also know how to proceed when the order is given.*

You have selected your places of refuge, and prepared for what lies ahead. The harvest will start quickly and last for only a few short weeks. At the end of it, many of this planet's excess passengers will have departed. And the Earth will be green again. The seas will recover. The air will brighten. Those of us who are left will— along with our friends and families—have a new beginning. More land. More space. A plentiful supply of fresh air and fresh water. Mankind is the disease, my friends. We are the cure.

These last two sentences were looped so they repeated four times, getting slightly louder with each iteration: MANKIND IS THE DISEASE, MY FRIENDS. WE ARE THE CURE. Beatrice glanced over at Lucas Todd. The normally relaxed face, so fit and tan, had turned an odd shade of white, and there was sweat on the man's forehead.

The crowd was deathly quiet. Unnerved, maybe. Somehow there was a lull in the music coming from other stages as well, and the loudest sound was the breath of the looming storm.

Ban MacAvoy again: "Friends, this is not a joke. The man in the video you've just seen is a contractor for the government of the United States. Remember his name.

Lucas Todd. What he's talking about is a plan to brutally murder millions of people… No, wait a minute. Let this sink in. He's talking about a plan to murder *billions* of people all over the world through the calculated and well-planned release of weaponized strains of disease. We're talking about the nastiest, most virulent plagues ever seen on this planet, guaranteed to lead to painful and humiliating deaths for our brothers and sisters on every continent. Share this video! We're streaming it now to as many people as we can. This needs to be seen. This needs to be STOPPED! I want to call my friend Paul Geiger out here now. Paul, come on out."

Paul Geiger strode out onto the stage, wincing at the weight of several thousand gazes. By his side was Lester White Bull, looking small and slight and distinctly uncomfortable. But also, Beatrice thought, fantastically brave.

"Paul, can you tell us what we just saw?"

The bespectacled biologist ran his hand back through his mop of white hair. "Thank you Ban. I sure can. But before I do, let me introduce a very important friend of mine. This is Lester White Bull. Lester unwittingly worked with the man you just saw in this video clip, Lucas Todd, on developing a plan to exterminate huge portions of the world's population. And if I'm not mistaken, Mr. Todd himself may be in the audience as well. Lucas, where are you? Come up and join us, won't you? Maybe you can explain how the hell it is you—"

Before Paul Geiger could even finish the sentence, Lucas Todd pulled a pistol from his jacket and leveled it at the stage. Mila saw him, and lunged to push his arm up. The pistol went off harmlessly, but now there were screams in the crowd. One of the security men brought the butt of his firearm down on Mila's skull, and the Russian girl fell to the grass.

Paul Geiger pointed at Lucas Todd, who was standing just behind Beatrice.

"There he is!" he said. "THERE!"

Two more shots rang out from just a few feet away, unbelievably loud in Beatrice's ears. She winced and ducked and realized that the gunfire had come from one of the two security men she didn't recognize. Up on stage, Lester White Bull doubled over. The crowd panicked. Men and women stumbled over each other as they scrambled to escape the vicinity.

The security men bunched tighter, penning their captives, but there was dissent in their ranks.

"Dude!" said Thor to Lucas Todd. "Was that for real? What are you doing?"

"Shut up," said Todd. "Keep these kids in line."

"Don't panic!" shouted Ban MacAvoy from the stage, though he sounded terrified himself. "Somebody call the police! NOW!"

One of the two new security men again leveled his weapon at the stage, this time aiming for MacAvoy. Black Panther leapt at him and the two men wrestled for control of the pistol.

Lucas Todd spoke into his wrist.

"Extraction!" he snapped. "We've got a situation. Send the bird!"

Mila was hoisted to her feet. She was conscious, but bleeding from a nasty cut above her left eye. Chantel broke loose for a moment, but she was tackled by one of Todd's thugs and dragged back by both legs to the group. Lucas Todd held his pistol to the back of Sanjay's head.

In the distance a helicopter appeared, wreathed in the advancing rain.

"Listen, goddammit!" said Todd. "That's enough. You're coming with ME! All of you! Nobody moves until I say so!"

"The hell I am," said Chantel. She lurched to her feet and broke away from the group again. This time one of the goons raised his pistol and fired. Chantel spun and staggered, but kept moving. Two steps later, she collapsed. Victor ran to help her.

Beatrice could hear sirens now. She saw two uniformed Austin police officers sprinting toward them from the far side of the meadow.

The helicopter moved fast. It was a big black aircraft, military in design, a vision of darkness and mechanized death. What was it called? Frankie would know. A *Blackhawk*. That was it. Even now it was starting to descend toward the lawn in front of the Toshiba stage. Beatrice watched as Lucas Todd glanced around him. He was frantic, now, and more dangerous than ever. But he must have realized his plan was crumbling. Finally he gave up. He uttered one last profanity before he and his two loyal security men ran for the Blackhawk, leaving their hostages behind.

Thor hesitated, but declined to join them. He went instead to where Chantel Griggs lay in the grass. He and Victor turned her over, checked her pulse, and started to perform mouth-to-mouth. Black Panther and Sanjay tended to Mila. Lightning flashed south of the lake, splitting the sky and sending a wave of thunder sweeping over the festival grounds. The great lawn of Zilker Park, formerly seething with people, was rapidly emptying.

Beatrice sprinted to the stage and pulled herself up. Ban MacAvoy and Paul Geiger were kneeling over Lester, who was bleeding from a wound in his chest. Lester's eyes were open, but he didn't seem to be able to see. The first few drops of rain were cold, but Beatrice felt warmth on her hands. It took her a moment to realize it was Lester's blood.

"Lester," she said. "Hey. Lester. Please."

Lester turned his head slightly. He fixed his gaze on Beatrice, and a moment later he smiled—a little ghost of a smile, like the last line of light in a winter sky.

"Bea," he whispered. "We didn't make it."

"Shhh. Be still. Don't talk."

"Hogwarts," he added. Then he closed his dark eyes and his grip relaxed and he was gone. Beatrice leaned so close to her friend that one of her tears landed on Lester's cheek.

"Hold on, Lester!" said Paul. "Hold on! The paramedics are on their way."

Beatrice didn't say anything, but she knew it was too late. She laid Lester's hand on his chest and stood up. She could see the storm bearing down on the field like a wave approaching a beach. Just a few yards away, several people were crouched beside Chantel Griggs, who was kicking her left leg out and back, fighting against the pain. Mila was beside them, talking to Chantel, but even from here Beatrice could see the blood that smeared Mila's face.

Twenty-five yards beyond her friends, the helicopter started to rise. Beatrice spotted Lucas Todd staring out at her from the door on one side of the airship, and she almost choked on her rage. Rain lashed her face and neck as she stood at the edge of the stage. The lightning flickered and danced in the clouds but she knew it wouldn't hurt her. In fact, it seemed to be *part* of her. She closed her eyes so she could see or feel the anger welling up inside her and for a moment she couldn't tell if the storm inside was creating the one around her or if it was the other way around or if it even mattered. She hadn't felt anything like this since the night she climbed high in the night sky over Galveston Bay, scouting for the hateful creature that menaced her family. But the feeling was back. It was bigger. It was humming inside her and she knew she was an ember blown by the wind, a sudden spark, a flash of light.

She screamed.

The world went quiet. There was a low scraping sound, almost as if the clouds had shape and weight and were rolling over each other like animals in some colossal death struggle. Then lightning lit up the sky as a bright tongue of white struck the helicopter with an ear-splitting crack. Two hundred feet up, the airship's main rotor coughed and quit. The aircraft seemed to hang motionless in the sky for a moment, still trying to climb, before the laws of physics took over. The Blackhawk plummeted to earth and landed with a ferocious shriek of folding metal.

A moment later, the fire broke out.

Fourteen: The Cloud

Lester White Bull was laid to rest on the Pine Ridge Reservation in South Dakota on a sunny October afternoon. A warm breeze, rare this time of year, tousled the prairie grass like an affectionate older brother.

Beatrice stood at the rear of a group of a dozen people who'd gathered to pay their respects. One man, introduced to her as a chief of the Oglala Sioux tribe, asked her if she wanted to say a few words as part of the ceremony. Paul Geiger and Chantel Griggs encouraged her. Chantel was still recovering from the bullet wound in her shoulder. She said she'd have tried to pay tribute to Lester if it weren't for the fact that she felt like she was going to pass out every five minutes or so.

Anne McIlvaine looked on with concern. She'd insisted on traveling to the funeral with her daughter, and in fact she'd kept her in sight just about every moment since they'd been reunited. She knew this couldn't last—Beatrice wasn't ordinarily the type to let anyone hover—but she was going to make the most of it while she could. Privately Anne suspected Beatrice needed a month or two of bed rest before she even tried to talk about the events of the last few days. She was back at home, but she was still anxious. She jumped when she heard the garbage truck outside. She mostly sat in her room and tried to rest. She was good at making herself scarce, even though the duplex was tiny. Sometimes, in fact, it seemed like she simply disappeared. Beatrice and Jennifer Ramos talked at least twice a day, occasionally for hours. But it broke Anne's heart to realize that Beatrice didn't have any friends at school who cared enough to call or text her. Her little girl just didn't seem to *belong* anymore. Anne wanted to shout at someone. She wanted to take the world by the collar and shake it and tell it just how beautiful and kind and miraculous her child was and would always be. But she was quiet, and she just nodded when Beatrice politely declined the Sioux chief's offer to speak.

The fact was, Beatrice had barely known Lester, and she felt like it would be wrong to pretend otherwise. She bowed her head and said a prayer instead. It wasn't a particularly good prayer. She knew that. But she said goodbye to Lester and told him and whoever else was listening that she had enjoyed making his acquaintance. That she felt the world was missing out on something special now that he was gone, and that she was grateful he'd liked her even if he hadn't really known her and why liking her wasn't a particularly brilliant idea anyway, given that she was a freak and had red hair and wasn't going to get a whole lot taller and had a brain that broke things.

Those who attended the funeral reported later that they saw a white buffalo drifting across the watery blue sky as the ceremony came to an end. A *cloud*, said skeptics. There were cumulus clouds cluttering the heavens that day, and cumulus clouds can look like all kinds of things. Still, the few people who were there to mourn Lester's passing saw what they saw. Beatrice smiled to herself when she heard the reports. She wasn't much of an artist. She knew that. She'd done the best she could.

Fifteen: Aftermath

The government issued denials.

Of course.

Admittedly, the Academy was a real place—and now a really *crowded* place, as broadcast, print, and internet media types flocked to the Pacific Northwest in an attempt to add authenticity to their coverage by standing dramatically just outside the facility's gates.

But there was nothing sinister about the Academy, said the spokespeople. It was an institution run by a private nonprofit group that worked with the federal government to identify and educate bright young foster children from around the world. Several of its alumni were accomplished and productive college graduates. One, for example, was now an engineer for Google. Another did statistical analysis for Lockheed Martin. And yes, Lucas Todd was a government contractor and Harvard-trained pediatric psychiatrist whose job was to recruit young men and women of exceptional intellectual ability for education at the Academy. But as for anything other than that: the man was a rogue ideologue who had managed to foment a dangerous international plot entirely on his own. His views by no means reflected the views of the United States government. Other nations—

most notably Russia, Germany, and China—were similarly tight-lipped. They deplored the evil represented by Lucas Todd and his network of associates in the governmental and military establishments of so many countries, but of course they denied knowledge of the plot or any involvement of its people.

But it was too late. The images shown at ACL Fest had gone out on a thousand cell phones. By seven p.m. that evening, the YouTube video REAL LIFE THANOS CONSPIRACY REVEALED had been viewed seven million times. An hour later, the figure was sixteen million, and climbing. Climbing rapidly. Thirty million. Forty-five million. By mid-morning of the next day, seventy-five million people around the globe had seen the brief clip of Lucas Todd exhorting his secret society to mass murder. The pressure for investigation was too intense to be ignored. First, China found evidence of the involvement of nine of its officials in its Ministry of National Defense. The Russians admitted their interior minister appeared to be implicated. And in Sao Paolo, Brazil, two prominent senators were filmed being led from their offices in handcuffs.

Lucas Todd never made it to trial. He died of his injuries in Austin's Seton Hospital. Two of his security men died as well, though the helicopter pilot survived the crash with only a broken leg and a severe concussion. Three other members of the Academy's security team were cornered in an office building in Round Rock, Texas and died in a gun battle with police. Thor and Black Panther turned themselves in to authorities and gave up everything they knew. It wasn't much, but it helped paint the picture of a huge international conspiracy that was able to hide behind the benign guise of a quiet experimental school in the forests of Washington State. In all, almost two hundred people were arrested in connection with the plot—half of this number being high-level employees and officials of the governments of the United States, Russia, and China. Several hundred caches of weaponized bacteria were recovered and neutralized, according to the press. And life on Earth went on in all its aimless, glorious confusion and beauty.

Back in Texas, Larry Bartkowski was indicted on multiple counts of kidnapping, assault, and false imprisonment and, in connection with Lucas Todd's shooting of Lester White Bull, being an accessory to capital murder. Anne McIlvaine was hugely angry; mildly heartbroken; and more than a little embarrassed. But heartbreaks heal. She and Beatrice and Frankie stayed in the duplex on Belgrove Avenue. They locked the doors and drew the shades and shut themselves up tight until the photographers and TV trucks finally disappeared to follow some new catastrophe and it was safe to drive to H-E-B again. Beatrice finally got past one particular column in the house of her sorrows and adopted a new cat, a rescue she named, predictably, Lester. And she was settling back into a more or less normal life when, one Saturday in December, the doorbell rang.

"Redheaded girl," said Mila Konradi, opening the door before Beatrice could get to it. "I am invited in, yes?"

"Of course. Mila. What--?"

Mila paused. She dropped her cigarette and ground it out on the cement of the front porch. "I come on errand, to speak at you."

"Yes, come in. Can I offer you some air freshener?"

"Again with the jokes. Trust me. I am laughing on inside."

"I'm just kidding." Beatrice was still feeling emotional. She couldn't help herself. She took two steps forward and wrapped Mila in a bear hug. "I'm glad you're here."

"Truly?"

"Truly. Because I've been thinking. You always dissed Hogwarts, and magic, and sentiment of all sorts, right? And the notion that a school could be founded on inherited traits like wizarding ability."

Mila raised her arms out wide. She shrugged. "I did so, yes. This is true. I am preparing to make successful arguing again."

"But my question is, what is so different about the Academy? You all are selected on the basis of your intellectual abilities, right?"

"Correct, inquisitive ginger person. I sense exercise of previously underused reasoning capacities, and am grudgingly exciting."

"And those abilities are inherited, correct?"

"This is such as all studies indicate."

"So who's the *wizard* in this story? And who's the muggle? Don't you see? You're living in a fairy tale too—one that's just as unfair, arbitrary, and undemocratic as anything the British could dream up."

Mila's eyes dropped for a moment. She pursed her lips. "Ah. Yes. You make interested point. I am symbolically relegating you to inferior status on basis of genetic factors beyond your controlling, just as muggles in stories of Harry Potter, Magical Capitalist Wizarding Boy. Except you are too somewhat late."

"What does that mean?"

"Paul Geiger is in charge of Academy now. And Paul Geiger does not want to do things similar to such as done before. All admittances to schooling will be voluntary, and subject to applicable law and fiats. Students will be encouraged to retain or establish ties with family, even if family is remote and possessed of questionable intellectual capacities. No more robot fights, and no more sorting into residence pods according to Human Aspirational Algorithm Technology, which is outdated anyway. Athletic funding will be subject to Title IX, as it should have been from the start. But more important: Science must be joined with softer, squishier types of thinking. No longer will students just be people of enormous genius such as myself. Also we will be taking normal individuals with swollen, bulging creativity and extravagant heart-strengths. And very strange people such as you."

"Wait a second. So when you say 'we,' you mean you're going back? I thought you hated the Academy."

"Correct in both statements. I am going back because things will be better. And because you are invited too, and you will be also better-making."

"I will? I mean...I *am*?"

"You are!" said Sanjay, appearing in the doorway. From the headset he wore, it was apparent he'd been listening in on the conversation. He wasn't shy about giving Beatrice a long, lingering hug. Chantel Griggs nearly broke Bea's back with the strength of her embrace. And even Victor Cho stepped forward to congratulate Beatrice, though he preferred to keep the touching to a minimum.

Beatrice noticed her mother and Frankie had entered the room as well. They stood staring at her, smiling, as Beatrice blushed.

"Well," said Beatrice. "I'll have to talk to my mom."

"No need," Mila answered. "She already knows."

Beatrice locked eyes with her mother. They didn't need to speak. Slowly, almost imperceptibly at first, her mother nodded.

But no silence was safe in the presence of the blue-haired Russian.

"Mother of Beatrice," said Mila. "Why do you cry?"

The End

Made in the USA
Coppell, TX
16 December 2021